TOKEN 2
MAKE IT REIGN

DIMITRA KITTLES

Table of Contents

CHAPTER: 1

Six hours is how long the drive was to get to the women's prison that housed Token. The twenty-foot bob-wired fence emulated a cage for wild animals surrounding the compound. As Reign pulled closer to the gate, she couldn't help the tears that streamed from her eyes. She drove up and down the newly paved lot until she spotted a park near a Nissan Maxima and whipped her Chevy Tahoe in it. She knew she had to pull herself together without delay. She felt herself falling apart and knew her sister would also sense it. Her thoughts were demented. There was no doubt Reign had seen her sister since she'd been locked up, but that was the county jail. People go in and out of the county all the time, and that alone gave hope that Token wouldn't go to prison. They prayed daily that the judge would overturn the verdict, but he didn't. She is in federal prison on a five-year bid.

Reign sat in her SUV for a minute for the sound of Maxwell to fade before removing the key from the ignition. She pulled out her Mac finishing powder to dab on her flawless face to mask the tear stains and the look of sadness. She knew if Token even sensed that she was upset, it would upset Token. It would be more of a sign of weakness, and in no way did she want her sister to think she wasn't tough enough to hold it down.

Reign took a deep breath and jumped out of her truck. She hit the alarm and approached the crowded entrance, where everyone waited to go through a checkpoint. Once through security, C.O. led Reign to a room filled with female inmates and their families. She walked in, looking for that one familiar face. Then she spotted it, but the only problem was that it was no longer familiar.

Token sat off at a table on the side, waiting patiently. When Reign walked over to the table, Token jumped up to hug her sister, almost causing her to fall backward. "Reign, you look great! The college has to have many cuties," she joked.

"Or is this new look for me?" Token cracked a smirk. She was referring to Reign's makeover, which Chasity highly influenced. Gone were the days of the Jill Scott naturals. Reign was rocking the best Indigo weaves money could buy. She had even begun wearing makeup but kept it light. Nothing too heavy. It was more about enhancing her beautiful dark-skinned features, not changing them.

Finally, they broke loose from the embrace. Reign carefully studied Token. The polished dime piece she remembered had been reduced to a Cleo from a *Set It Off* look-a-like. Reign was in disbelief.

"Reign!" Token snapped. She was taking Reign right out of her thoughts. "What's the matter? What are you thinking about?"

Reign shook her head and uttered nothing as she searched for her sister in front of her. Token took a seat, and Reign followed. The seven big cornrows Token sported kept Reign's attention until she finally spoke. "What happened to your face?"

"Listen, don't worry about that. Just know this ain't no walk in the park."

"Man, this ain't fair." Reign began to sob but was quickly interrupted by Token.

"Look, life ain't fair." Token leaned over the table, drawing herself closer to Reign's face. "LOOK AT ME, REIGN. WE'RE BROKE!" Token whispered, focusing on Reign's expression. The money I left should be long gone, if not very well on its way."

"I know TK. Chastity and I are doing our best. But it's hard to juggle school and working 40 hours a week. Reign's eyes shifted downwards.

"FUCK A JOB." Token's voice raised.

Reign flinched.

Then Token quickly remembered where they were and adjusted her anger before the C.O. caught wind of her frustration and ended her visit. "Listen, Reign, I need you to step up your game. There is plenty of work out there, but you have to be willing to go hard for me like I did for you. I need you. I need you, little sis." Token went from persuading to conning in a matter of seconds. "Look at me. I'm hungry."

Tears filled up in Reign's eyes.

"Are you willing to grind for me—for us?" Her voice returned to sincerity, or at least it seemed that way for the moment. It would be best if you did anything to hold us down. If the tables were turned, you wouldn't want anything, Reign.

Sad but true. Token would do anything and everything for her sister. She was always willing to be that sacrificial lamb, but Reign was no Token. She didn't have it in her. She was clear on book knowledge, but the street game was another ball game for Reign, and Token knew it. She knew this was going to be a risk. But she didn't care. She wanted to live in prison like she lived on the outs. She knew she wouldn't be respected, living like a homeless person with no family. She considered herself a Boss chick on the streets, but to everyone who sees her now, they think she's a fucking nobody, and that was not the case.

Reign sat there motionless, listening to everything Token had to say. She glanced around the room, watching all the women dressed in blues, and couldn't imagine trading places with them, but she didn't want to disappoint her big sister, her mentor, and her idol. She loved her too much and didn't want to let her down.

Once Token regained Reign's attention, she started teaching her codes for their telephone conversations and used the remainder of the visit to teach her about the banking business. Token spoke low, and when someone would come near, she would quickly change the subject. Reign was hanging on to Token's every word, making it her business to execute this plan to the fullest. She wanted nothing more than for her sister to believe in her. When it was time to leave, the C.O.s lined up all the inmates by last name. They responded with their state-issued ID number and disappeared. Reign was eager to go after she watched her sister be led off like a real criminal. That's when she realized Token had fallen from grace, and it was her time to Reign.....

CHAPTER: 2

The ride home was a little more relaxing than the one going up. It was five o'clock, and Reign wasn't due to arrive back in front of her door for another three hours. She reached the rearview mirror to hit the OnStar button, then instructed it to call Chastity.

"Ho-la."

"Let me find out you think you're bilingual," Reign said, laughing into the speakers at Chasity's broken Spanish.

"How was the visit? How does she look? Did she cry?"

"Hold up, hold up. Take a breath, for God's sake. I'll fill you in on the entire visit when I get home because I don't want to burn up these expensive minutes."

"Where is your cell?" Chasity asked.

"I couldn't bring it to the prison, so I left it in the car with the apps open by mistake, and it drained my battery, which, by the way, my charger is in the Benz."

"I know. I saw it in there earlier," Chasity interrupted.

"Well, my call was to tell you not to wait for me. I have to make a pit stop before bringing it in," Reign explained.

"It must be nice to have late nights. When I grow up, I want to be just like you," Chasity jokes.

"Whatever, big head. Don't forget to walk the dogs. I'll see you later."

"Ok. Smooches, Sis."

"Yep, back at you." On Star ended the call, and music returned to the Bose speakers.

While driving down 27, Reign couldn't help but think about her conversation with Token. Although she worked hard to become a lawyer, maybe it was time to put that dream on hold. Her mind went back and forth, flirting with the thoughts of becoming that chick.

Reign finally arrived at her destination. It was now 8:45 p.m., and she was exhausted. She wanted nothing more than to go home and sleep, but she knew this visit was necessary. She pulled her SUV up into the marble roundabout behind the black Bugatti with the plates that read: The Peoples Champ.

Reign stepped out of the truck, fighting for strength for her fragile legs pinned beneath the wheel for almost 7 hours. She made her way to the French doors and rang the bell. The sound of the chimes playing inside the gates was soothing. The door slowly opened.

"Hey, Babe." Reign couldn't help but fall into these arms. Besides, she'd become accustomed to them since the words 'five years' fell off the judge's lips. "Come on, Reign. You have to do better than this." His compassion had become addictive to Reign. She never meant for things to go this far, but because they shared this common bond, it was easy for this to happen.

CHAPTER: 3

"Hello."

"Good morning. This is Charles Westerman, Branch Manager of Bank of America. May I speak with Chastity Beoutche?"

Chasity had to hurry and readjust her sleepy voice to an alert, professional one. "This is her. Good morning, Mr. Witterman."

"Ms. Beoutche, I have your resume in front of me, and I wanted to know if you were available for an interview."

"Yes! Sure. Will that be today?" Chasity gleamed with excitement.

"Yes. Let's shoot at 2:00 PM."

"Yes, sir. Two PM sounds great. I'll see you then."

"Thank you, Ms. Beoutche. I look forward to meeting you."

Chasity hit the end button and then jumped excitedly as if she had already gotten the job. Her first thought was to run to her closet to find something to wear. Going through tons of name brands, she finally came across a winner. She glanced at the time on the cable box, which read 10:05 AM. She had plenty of time, she thought to herself.

She hurried out of her room to the family room to let the pups out of their kennels. "Juicy, get down." She always had to yell at Token's badass puppy, who was spoiled and missed Token just as Chastity and Reign did. Juicy was the youngest and the friskiest of the trio. She excitedly jumped from chair to chair, anticipating the door opening for their morning walk. Chasity grabbed the leashes, connected them to their collars, scooped up her keys, and headed out the door.

Determined to make her interview on time, she rushed to the dog park and let the pups loose. While waiting for them to handle their business, Chas texted Reign, who hadn't made it home yet, telling her all the good news.

When she looked to put her phone back on the clip on her pajamas, she glanced across the street and saw L's Escalade drive by. Chas was caught off guard. Her eyes followed without her brain's permission. The tints on the windows made it difficult for her to see the driver, but judging from the silhouette, she could tell it was a chick pushing his whip that she once drove. Not wanting to get down on herself or start those thoughts back up of L, she quickly whistled for the pups, gathered them up, and walked back to the house.

Once back in, she poured them food and water and trotted back to her room to prepare for her interview. Chas hopped in the shower in her bathroom to wash the pup smell off her body. She got out, dried off, and turned the music on for motivation. She needed to hear hardcore fuck a dude type of shit to keep her spirits up. Nikki Minaj came through the speakers, and that's all she needed. It took her less than 10 minutes to get dressed. She pushed her hair up into a bun and felt ready to win.

When she sat on the side of her bed to put on her strapped-up red Valentino Stilettos, Ms. Reign had walked into her room unannounced. "Are you going to an interview for a job or a date?" Reign giggled as she stood in the doorway, watching Chasity get dressed.

"Well, welcome home, and what's wrong with what I'm wearing?" Chasity second-guessed herself.

"Nothing wrong with it. Suppose you were going to the club or on a date. Take that off. I'll be right back. I'm glad I made it back before you left the house." Chasity could hear Reign's voice disappearing down the hall. Chasity peeled off the T-strap black mini dress that showed off all her prize possessions and returned to her closet to try again.

"BAM!" Reign yelled over the music, showing off the black two-piece, double-breasted Donatella Versace suit with matching black and white 4-inch heels. "This is what you need."

"I never seen you in that," Chasity said as she looked over the suit.

"That is because I preserved for my more professional moments. This is something every woman has to have."

"You have a point." Everything Chasity had done in her life consisted of her being sexy. Reign stayed in the room to help put the picture together. When she was done, you could see a significant transformation. The suit fit as if it was tailor-made for Chasity. She filled it out better than Reign on any day.

Reign then sat Chas down at her vanity and brushed her hair up in a neater bun than Chas had thrown up there. Chasity looked amazing. Reign was brilliant and wise beyond her years. She rehearsed several standard interview questions before she wished Chas luck and sent her on her way.

CHAPTER: 4

Reign woke up to the smell of tacos and enchiladas. The clock on her nightstand read 4:59 PM. She had dozed off after Chas left for her interview. She got up to use the bathroom and hadn't realized how sore her pussy was until now. Damn, dude hurt the NaNa. She gasped as she wiped her irritated vagina. Afterward, she washed her face and hands and joined Chas, who was cooking something.

When she reached the bottom step, Reign watched from a distance as Chas emulated the woman on the cooking show that appeared on the 6-inch flip-screen TV that hung underneath the cabinet. "Ah, Rachel Ray!"

"Shit. Girl, you scared me!"

"Girl, you need to be more aware of your surroundings because someone is always scaring you."

"No, chick. Someone always creeping up on me." Chas laughed as she continued to stir the food.

"Whatever. Anyway, how did the interview go?"

"I'm not sure," Chasity said, shrugging her shoulders but not taking her eyes off the TV screen.

"What do you mean? I'm not sure." Reign quizzed.

"Well, the man was nice, but he never said yay or nay, so how was I supposed to know?" Normally, Reign would clown anyone who spoke like this, but Chas would get a pass because this was her truth.

Chasity had never had a job, so Reign felt terrible for being a little hard on her by forgetting the golden rule: common sense isn't common.

"My bad, chick, I forgot to tell you how proud I am of you for even landing the interview. If you followed my instructions on what to say, then there is no doubt you have it."

"AWWWWW. That's so sweet, Reign."

"Here, Taste some of this." Chasity grabbed the wooden spoon, put the meat sauce on it, and placed it in Reign's mouth.

"Damn, this is good." Reign smacked her lips together and watched Chas style and profile at the sound of Reign's compliments. "Just think, the next man is going to have the full package," Reign jokes, but it wasn't funny to Chas.

"Speaking of which, I saw a girl driving L's truck today."

"Who? The tall, light-skinned chick with blonde and brown hair?"

"What? You know about her?" Chas's eyes begin to water.

"No," Reign answered. "I just saw her occasionally rolling through, and they get out of his car one day. Anyway, who cares? You have to move on. L is a paid *hoe*, but he's a hoe. You deserve so much more. You'll realize you made the right choice. He's just going to use and abuse her, and when he finishes, he'll toss her in the closet like an old rag doll." Reign's voice spoke with disgust. "Now, let's prepare for these big-time bankers and brokers about to come your way." She massaged Chas's shoulders as if you were preparing for a big fight.

"Yeah, I guess you're right. It is time for me to move on."

"That's my girl. Let's grab plates to chill out, eat, and be fat."

"Speak for yourself." Chas laughed as she pinched Reign's stomach.

CHAPTER: 5

It was early Saturday afternoon, and Reign took the dogs out to check the mail with her. The box was full because they only checked it once a week. On her way back, she watched as L's Escalade flew by. He needed to get a grip. Reign was under the impression that L was trying to taunt Chastity. He was beginning to appear desperate. She guessed he figured Chas would have been crawling back to him by now. And the truth is, she would have had it not been for Reign and Token rescuing her. They constantly reminded her that she could do better and that she could do without him.

Reign returned the dogs to the house and tossed the mail on the counter. When one of the envelopes slid to the floor, it caught Reign's attention. The red letters that read URGENT caused her to open it even faster. It was a letter from the Orange County Tax Collector. It read that the taxes on the property were six months past due, and the balance was going up by the day.

Reign begins to panic. All she could think of was what Token said on her last visit. God knows she didn't want to trade places with her mentor. She didn't want to lose everything her sister had worked so hard for. Having no other choice, Reign went to the safe and counted out the last $11,000 they had. Token never told her about the taxes or association fees. She was learning all of this day by day.

Reign hurried to get dressed to take the money to the tax collector's office. When she pulled out of the driveway, she could see L's Escalade creeping in her direction. Both cars ended up at the four-way point at the same time. Not wanting to give L or his new *Little Trick* any energy, Reign turned her head in the opposite direction, looking at the swans in the nearby pond.

Beep! Reign heard the sound, but when she looked in the rearview, she saw that there wasn't anyone behind her. Beep! She heard the horn again but looked to her left this time. It was L with his window down, rolling solo. "What up?" he said, nodding his head up and down in Reign's direction. With one hand on the wheel, leaning to the side, Reign took her free hand and pointed to her chest, questioning his greeting.

"Are you talking to me?"

L removed his shades from his eyes. "Yeah, Ms. Lady. What's up with you?"

I know damn well this nigga knows who I am and knows Chas lives with me. Reign nodded and pulled off, heading out of the gated community. The nerve of these men. They think every chick is desperate. But I must admit that dude is fine with that little nappy fade cut. Reign laughed at herself and continued on her journey.

When she arrived at the tax collector's building, the shit was crowned as hell. Reign felt very uneasy traveling with $11,000 on her. She knew her nervousness would warrant suspicion; therefore, she tried her best to remain calm. She picked up her phone and texted someone special to ease her mind. She just wanted to catch up with him to see how things were going. By the time they finished their texting, she was at the counter. She handed the stubby white man with the gold-rimmed glasses the bill along with the $11,000 that she counted out carefully.

"Excuse me, ma'am. Don't you have a checkbook?"

An older white woman looked on and chatted from behind her. Reign didn't know how to respond to the nosy-ass lady, so instead, she tried to ignore her and keep on counting.

"I'm sorry, sir. I received this letter, and I panicked." Reign began to explain to the gentlemen who were assisting her. "Oh, no worries, ma'am. We get cash all of the time." He looked past Reign, mean-mugging the nosy-ass lady behind her.

"Now, you have a nice day, Ms. Davis." He handed Reign the receipt, and she exited.

CHAPTER: 6

Reign had felt uneasy about her next move since she'd left the tax collector's office several weeks prior. She wanted nothing more than to save everything Token had gone but found it quite impossible. All the funds had been depleted, and between her and Chasity, they could barely keep their heads above water. Reign had been doing a great job at keeping her pockets deep from her boo, but lately, he'd been fucking her insides out and sending her home empty-handed.

Until now, she was getting an allowance of $25,000 to $50,000 a month. Things had changed, and it was time to take her sister's advice and make things happen. She was trying to be patient and let the chips land as they may, but this was killing her. Had it been Token, she would have figured this out. If TK thought it, TK did it. Unfortunately, Reign was cut from a different cloth. Her hustle was different.

Chas and Reign sat at the table, trying to put the money together to pay the rest of their college tuition bills. "Shit, this is frustrating as hell. TK took on giants to provide for us, but now we can't even afford to send her stamps and envelopes. This is so messed up. Shit, I don't know about you, Chas, but I'm dropping out of school so I can make more money," Reign announced with her face in her hands.

"No, Reign, you can't do that. It would mean everything TK worked so hard for would be in vain. Now, we have to find a way to cake off without joining her. I was thinking about going back into modeling ." Chas laughed as she struck a pose.

"This shit ain't funny. This is my sister we're talking about. How about you leave the planning to me." Reign looked into Chas's eyes with seriousness.

"I think it's time."

"Time for what?" Chas retorted with a clueless look on her face.

"I think it's time to take over where Token left off."

"What are you talking about, Reign? Don't be silly. You have your entire life ahead of you. Don't blow it."

"I wasn't just speaking of me. I was talking about us." Reign looked at Chas to study her reaction.

Chasity wasn't beat for this. She knew she owed Token her life. But was she willing to jeopardize her young life for Reign, which was yet to be determined?

"Listen, I have the perfect plan. We are in an even better position than Token. Now that you work at the bank. How much better could it get?"

"Listen, Reign. I feel you and all, but..."

"BUT NOTHING!" Reign jumped to her feet, scaring her damn self. "My sister saved your ass from self-destruction." Reign spoke in a much calmer tone. "If it had not been for her…"

"What? I would be on the streets. Go ahead and say it." Reign and Chasity stood toe to toe.

"Your sister was a thief, Reign. It's not like she took her hard-earned money and fronted it for us."

Reign began to think. What Chas said was somewhat accurate but did not matter to her. Regardless of how Token did it, she made it happen, and she wasn't going to let this ungrateful, gold-digging half-breed come up on her sister's dime. Reign was referring to Chas's Mother being white and father being Black.

"If that's how you feel, that's you. But I can tell you this: my sister loved you like a sister. She wanted nothing but the best for you. And the only thing you can say is she's a thief? That's low—low—even for you."

Chas didn't mean for this to go so far. She knew TK loved her. Reign was right. They needed to step up their game, and she was perfectly positioned. "Look, I'm sorry. I was out of pocket for calling TK a thief." She looked over at Reign with those puppy dog eyes and walked closer to her for a hug.

Reign pretended to be stubborn. "Calling my sister a thief." She cracked a smile. "She's not a thief. She's more like a neighborhood, Robin Hood." They both cracked up in laughter as they embraced one another.

"I love you, lil sis." Chas kissed Reign's forehead.

"Little sis. We're only a year apart," Reign bragged.

"You're still my little sis as long as the big sis is away. Now let's get this money." They gave each other a high five and sat down to plan their next move.

CHAPTER: 7

The next day was a big day for Reign. She needed to be focused. She ignored all the phone calls from the night before. She didn't need any distractions. Today, she needed to be a sponge and absorb everything that could be an asset to her plan. Today was Reign's first day back at school. The plans had changed, and so did her major. She walked over to registration to pick up her schedule and syllabus. She was eager to know if she needed to complete any prerequisites or had already had enough to continue with the plan.

She took her well-manicured finger and scrolled down the page, and bingo, there it was. Reign was enrolled in Xavier Butler's Computer Science and Information Technology class. "YES!" Reign gleamed in excitement. This was it—the missing piece to the puzzle. Reign rushed to the room listed on the sheet, knowing she had little time to get this.

Once in the room, she took a seat. Judging from the looks of things, she seemed to be oblivious to this part of the world. The room was filled with geeks and techies. She didn't mind, however. She had a purpose, which alone kept her eyes on the grind. The class was a 3-hour block, and 2 1/2 was wasted with formalities and housekeeping rules.

While listening to *all of* Mr. X, as he preferred to be called, dry-ass jokes, Reign scanned the room, looking for the best candidate to complete her mission. She thought she spotted one, but it would be her next class before she would approach him.

The class was out for the day, and Reign wanted to stop at the nearest ABC liquor store on her way home to grab a bottle of Ciroc Coconut. Before moving to Florida, she was no drinker, but after the turn of events, she'd been drinking like a fish.

Reign pulled up in front of the house and realized the Benz was still gone. Chas was still at work or roaming the streets, which meant one of two things. When she walked in the door, she was met in complete silence. The pups never barked if they heard you typing in the alarm code. They just stayed still in their kennels until someone acknowledged them. Well, tonight wasn't that night. Reign tiptoed in the dark to get a glass to take to her room when she tripped over the runner on the walkway, causing the pups to sound off. "SHIT!" Okay, okay, calm down. I'll return to take you all for a walk in a few minutes." Reign continued to march to her room for a drink and a little solace. Hoping Chas would come in and take the pups out and feed them as she's done in the past.

It was 8:30 pm, and Chas still hadn't made it home. Reign couldn't believe she'd drunk the entire bottle of Ciroc. She was feeling good but needed a little air.

She exited her bed and put on black leggings, a white tank top, and a pair of Bebe slides. She then descended the steps and opened the kennels to let the pups out.

It wasn't until she hit the night air that she realized how intoxicated she was. She reached down to detach the diamond-studded collar off the girl and the gold link from the boy, and they zoomed off into the darkness. It's a good thing they were trained enough to know their boundaries. She stayed squatted down, trying to regain her composure, when a man's silhouette appeared behind her. "You iight shawty?" the deep voice asked.

"What is it about you? Do you have an alarm in our home that tells you when we step out?" She still felt slightly dizzy but didn't hesitate to reach for his hand to get up.

"I don't think we've formally met. I'm Jason Ta...."

"Yeah, yeah, yeah. I know who you are, silly. Your Chasity's ex-fiance," Reign replied while trying to make out the whereabouts of the pups.

Jason laughed before replying. "Oh, is that what she's telling y'all?"

"What do you mean by that what she's telling us?" Reign whistled for the pups.

"Look, Ms. Lady Chasity was my assistant, and that was it. Of course, I hit it occasionally, but only because it was convenient." He watched Reign sway from side to side, trying to maintain her balance.

Reign was surprised at his allegations but didn't want to give this buster any more of her time. "Well, I'm gonna say goodnight." She gathered the pups and began to walk away.

"I guess I'll chat with you later, Ms. Lady. Maybe one day you'll have time for the real 411 on you, girl," L hollered as Reign walked away. Reign waved her hand and kept on stepping.

It was now 10:00 p.m., and Chas still had not arrived home. Reign was getting worried. She reached over to her nightstand to call her. She let the phone ring until the voicemail picked up. This was unlike Chas, so Reign thought. But honestly, did she know Chas? Did she have another life?

Reign was still too drunk to put things together, so she slipped her tights back over her purple nightie and headed out the door. Reign walked up to the front door but felt butterflies in her stomach. She came to her senses and turned to walk away. Too late, the mahogany wood door crept open, and L's voice spoke. "Coming to see me?" he asked.

He was so cocky. Reign thought to herself. "I was wondering about Chas, and I thought you could help me. Chas had been acting differently lately, and who'd better explain her behavior than her ex-fiance, boss, or whatever?"

"I appreciate the visit for whatever reason," L blushed.

"Well, can I come in?"

"Damn, of course. How rude of me." Reign had never been in a mansion before. She was taken aback by how stunning the foyer was. "I was just enjoying a glass of Rose'. Would you care for some?"

"Sure." Although Reign had been drinking almost all day, she figured another glass wouldn't hurt. She sat down on the plush chocolate leather couch and began to consume more alcohol. For Reign, it felt a little awkward to be sitting there with L with no real explanation. She sat and looked at them as he looked back at her. They both were lost for words.

"So tell me why you're here?" L said in a very sexy tone.

Reign looked around at all the trophies and awards L had collected over the years and still hadn't come up with a decent response. "I want to know a little more about Chas," she responded with the same look of innocence that she does.

"Well, where do I start? She's a manipulator, a con artist, and the best head giver in town," he joked.

Reign didn't seem to be moved by his description of her friend. She thought maybe he was lying or perhaps he was jealous of her finally doing something without him. She didn't know what to believe. All she knew was that she was drunk as hell, and L was looking *better* than a mutherfucker at that moment. He had the most exotic ways to bring a girl to her knees, and that's precisely where Reign went with L's help.

L was only wearing a white fitted tee with a pair of Jordan joggers, which made it easy for him to slip his dick out and into Reign's mouth. It was big. It was tasty. Those were her thoughts as she continued to do the unmentionable. L stood directly before her as she began to work her head action. L's moans and groans only excited Reign. It caused her to go faster and harder, working her jaw muscles into overdrive, but she wasn't letting up.

L leaned over and started to tug at Reign's tights. It was pretty tricky to do in this position, so Reign assisted him. Once she got them entirely off, he began to play with her ass. He smacked it and made it jiggle. He then wet his thumb and placed it in her asshole. This turned her on even more, causing her juices to flow. That must've done it for L because he started cumming like a speeding bullet.

That was a complete letdown for Reign because she didn't get hers. She slowly pulled herself up and began pulling her tights back up when she noticed L lying on his back, massaging his manhood up and down. He then instructed her to have a seat on top of him.

Reign was surprised but not disobedient. She quickly removed her clothes, jumped on him, and began to ride. His dick was still lovely and intricate, sending pleasure up her spine.

This lasted for almost one hour before they both exploded. When they were done, Reign kindly put her clothes back on and let herself out without saying a word.

CHAPTER: 8

The second day of school was much better than the first. Today, she was prepared with the tools she needed. She wore one of Chasity's very revealing dresses with colorful peep-toe wedges. All eyes were on her as she made her way to the back of the class.

Mr. X stood firmly in front of the class as he watched her. "Ladies and gents, before we start our session today, I wanted to take note of our advanced techies versus the beginners. Now, that's by far not taking shots. I want to make sense of what's in front of me. Make sense?"

Reign surveyed the room and listened for everyone's response. Hers was simple. She didn't have a clue. Although Reign knew little about the computer world, she watched and noted who did.

It was apparent when he spoke. Zachary Vander was Mr. Steve Jobs and Bill Gates himself. When he mentioned that he was a Mac guy and had been for over four years, she knew that he was her guy. When class broke for a break, Reign approached the water cooler, where a group of guys assembled.

Zak was the center of attention as he explained how he created many apps, and the listeners gave him their undivided attention. Reign squeezed through the crowd and excused herself. She listened as they continued and placed a Dixie cup under the spout to catch some water. She dropped the cup. "OH MY GOD! I'm so sorry," she claimed, bending her backside over in Zak's direction to pick up the cup.

Everyone jumped back, trying not to get wet. "Here, let me help you." Zak reached for Reign's hand. His blue eyes caught a glimpse of how sexy Reign was.

"Hi, I'm Zachary, by the way." He introduced himself in a shy tone.

"Hi, Zachary. I'm Reign."

"Please to meet you." He stared at her as if he'd seen a ghost.

"I'm very sorry about wetting up your shoes. How can I make it up to you?" Reign flirted. Zak's face turned beet red, but he just smiled. She knew from there that this would be a walk in the park.

CHAPTER: 9

"**N**EXT!"

"Good morning," Token spoke to the young miserable inmate on the other side of the canteen window."

"Tag, please."

Damn, this bitch has to be the unhappiest person in this world. I know this is a prison, but damn, Token thought to herself.

"0.00." The woman scanned her tag and gave it back.

Token grabbed her bag and walked away, swinging an empty canteen bag.

Tears slowly dropped out of her eyes as she returned to her dorm. Token's mind just went blank. She was scared, hungry, and now confused. She hadn't had money in her account in weeks. She knew Reign and Chasity were struggling but damn. She figured they would at least have enough to cover her for the first year or two. She couldn't believe they were broke already.

When the C.O. popped the door, Token walked into the dorm, making a beeline to the phone. After waiting her turn, she anxiously dialed home, but the number had been restricted. Like many other times, she tried, hoping it was some mistake.

After reality set in, she hung up the phone and went to sit on her bunk.

"Are you okay, sunshine?" the older woman named June, who lay in 6 lower, asked. Token was beat for conversation. She just wanted to get her pad and pen and write home without interruptions.

"Yep, I'm good." Token placed her belongings on the top bunk and hopped on her bed. She was hoping to make sense of this.

MEANWHILE, BACK AT THE RANCH

Chasity was tired as shit. She had spent a couple of nights with her boss. She hadn't told Reign she'd been sleeping with her boss. She knew Reign would disapprove. She knew she would form an opinion about her sleeping with a married man.

Chasity started her job not long ago as a part-time teller, only to be promoted to a personal banker in a matter of weeks. She had little experience in that department but a lot in another. Chasity had quit school altogether. She figured the money she had made and the bonuses Mr. Witterman had hit her off with were enough to leave school. When Reign first spoke of it, she was against it, but once the money started rolling in, she didn't consider it.

On the other hand, Chasity took Reign's advice and began learning the system. Determined to master the banking system, she attended every training class and daily workshops.

Chasity brought home $6,000 today and laid it on the table for Reign to see when she entered the door. She knew that wasn't a lot, but it was enough to help them keep the lights on. Chas went into the kitchen and pulled the all-clad pots and pans that hung above the island to cook a much-needed dinner. She popped on the T.V. and heard the breaking news of an Orlando woman killing her husband she suspected of cheating.

Chas turned that off with the quickness. She didn't want any parts of that.

"Hey, chica. How have you been?" Reign wasted no time, so she entered the door and headed straight for Chasity.

"I'm good," Chas responded, motioning to the cash on the table.

"Girl, don't tell me you've been on the hoe stroll." Reign joked but was serious. There was no telling, especially after what L had told her.

"Call it what you want, but the bottom line is we have some money to send Token."

Reign walked over, picked up the money, and began counting it. She started smiling when she passed 3,000 and was still counting. Once she finished, she rushed to Chas for a hug. Chas was gazing at the pan with olive oil and was caught off guard by Reign's embrace. "This is all good, Chas, but we need to talk." Reign washed her hands and began helping Chas prepare dinner.

By nine o'clock, they had cooked, eaten, cleaned up, and discussed how they were about to move. Chasity discussed how the banking system works with Reign. Reign was glad to see Chas was taking this seriously, but she needed to know if she could trust her. On one hand, she thought she could, but on the other....she wasn't too sure.

Her first plan was to test Chasity's loyalty. Reign was no Token, but she wasn't green either. She knew enough that if Chasity had efficiently completed this first task, they would be good and paid by Easter.

BANKROLL

Reign rolled up to Chasity's job. It was a Friday afternoon, and the place was packed. She sat in the waiting area and watched for Chas to make eye contact. She did. Reign moved to Chasity's office, sat on the far left, and took a seat. Chas spoke as if they'd never seen one another before. Reign was confused. Why the fuck was Chas acting so bubbly and dumb?

Reign just reached into her purse and pulled out a $22,000 check. Chas pranced around her desk, calling Reign "Mrs. Franklin" for her entire time there. She walked out to the vault and counted out $22,000 in cash. When she got back in the room, Mr. Witterman accompanied her.

Reign was shaking in her 6-inch heels. Why the fuck would she bring him back? I know damn well this bitch isn't setting me up. Mr. Witterman introduced himself by extending his hand. Reign was lost. She'd forgotten the name that quick of whom Chas was calling her. After he shook her hand, he quickly exited, and Chas sat back at her desk, counting out the money. Reign's eyes grew bigger and bigger.

She couldn't believe she was about to walk out with that kind of money. She waited for Chas to give her the ok to put it in her tote and leave the premises. And just like that, she did. Reign made it to the car with sweat dripping everywhere. Her nerves were wrong, and she couldn't help but believe they had done it. But not before looking in every direction for the police. This was too good to be true. If this was this easy, she was ready to return for more.

She started home, watching her back, hoping she would get there safely. When Reign pulled into her subdivision, she noticed L's truck approaching her. Trying hard not to look in his direction, she began playing with the radio. Both SUVs passed one another, and Reign felt relieved.

She hadn't spoken with L since the night they had sex, and she wanted to keep it that way. That night she was drunk and horny. That's all. There is nothing else to it. And now that Chasity is entirely on board with getting money, she doesn't want to jeopardize their relationship.

When she pulled to the house, she first walked to the community mailbox to retrieve their mail. There were bills, bills, and more—and a letter from Token. This time, she was eager to open all of it. When she reached the door, she couldn't wait to get inside.

She was anxious to know how TK was doing and wondered if she had received that $1000 they sent her. Once inside, she dropped everything onto the table except for TK's letter and headed for her room, ignoring the pups' barks. When Reign reached her room, she dumped all the money out of her tote and onto her bed.

She smiled at her accomplishments, knowing Token would be proud of her. She sat on the bed before the money, crossed her legs, and opened the letter. As she began to read, her smile disappeared. Token was going in on her. Reign couldn't believe what she was reading.

She thought she was doing good. She was doing her best at trying to hold it down. TK called her all types of coward bitches. Reign was furious. She looked at all the money they laid nearby and thought about picking it up and throwing it across the room, but she didn't. She had better plans.

Just then, Chasity walked into the room. "What's wrong?" Chasity immediately ran to Reign's aid. Reign didn't say anything. She just passed Chasity the letter. Reign watched as Chas's eyes followed the words on the page. Her facial expression began to change. Finally, she spoke. "WHAT THE FUCK! How dare she blame us for her shortcomings." She looked up at Reign. "No disrespect intended, baby sis, but we didn't imprison Token. She put herself in there. We're doing our best. But she's not my responsibility. Now, you can sit here and cry about it if you want to, but I'm not. Look!" Chasity pointed at the bed where the cash was. "We're doing our part. There is nothing to feel bad about." Chas made her way over to Reign for comfort.

Reign dried her eyes as she accepted Chasity's embrace. "Look, chick. Dry your eyes, and let's go shopping. It's plenty more where that came from."

They laughed as they separated, heading in different directions to get dressed as Reign ran her shower water. She thought about the words the Token was speaking in her letter. Although Chasity made sense, Token was right. Reign was a poor steward of her money. She had to show Token that she could make as much money as she did and live like a boss, but she needed more help.

Chapter: 10

There was no more time to waste. After Reign and Chasity went shopping and paid the remaining bills, money was getting low again. Reign listened to her voice messages on her phone and knew she needed to devise a plan. She dialed one of the callers back to arrange a date. Later that day, Reign pulled up at the Double Tree Hotel to meet her newfound friend.

She waltzed into the lobby and gave the front desk agent her reservation information. The agent smiled and then handed Reign her keys to her room. As she made her way to the room, her belongings trailed behind her. She finally reached the door and opened it to begin setting up the shop. She immediately unpacked her bags.

After about 15 minutes in the room, there was a knock. Reign opened the door, and in walked Zak. Every day was a new day to learn something from Zak. He and Reign had spent countless hours working together, both in and away from class.

But it wasn't until now that Reign needed him to teach her the illegal part of the operation, and she needed that to be done in total privacy. Zak was unaware of the damage he was about to cause. He was so passionate about knowing every computer operation on this side of the earth that he was oblivious to the trap.

Zack made himself readily available for Reign. He was at her every beck and call, and Reign knew if she knew she had Zak in her hand. Zak even put countless programs on her computer for free. He wasn't sure why she would need all of this. He knew she wanted to be more in tune with the new technology. Besides, he didn't care. He just wanted a chance to be in the presence of a beautiful woman.

Reign played her part. She was sure to change into something more revealing and watched Zak take a peep or two with excitement. She wasn't about to sleep with him or anything. She was putting on a show as he worked his magic.

This was pretty complex stuff to her, but to Zak, it was a piece of cake. He was done in a matter of minutes. Reign thanked Zak and saw him at the door. He walked out, thinking he should turn around, but it was too late. The door slammed behind him.

Reign was relieved Zak was gone. She had more work to do that didn't require his expertise. In fact, after learning about the banking system, different graphic design programs, and how to become her own company, he was pretty much not excited anymore. At this point, she'd thought she'd put her newfound skills to work.

She logged on to the IRS website and produced an EIN for the future. When she was done, she packed up her belongings and was ready to hit the road when her cell phone rang.

It was M. He wanted to know where she was. Although she didn't want to be bothered by him anymore, she knew he had plenty of money. She needed all the money she could get at this point in her life.

She hung up the phone and agreed to meet with him. They couldn't go too many places together in town because she couldn't be seen with him.

Reign had finally made it over to M's house. As she walked, she knew she had to play her role. She walked in and headed straight for the main suite. Confused, he followed. Reign knew why she was there this time. Everything from that point was a piece of cake when they entered the suite.

The bright sun peeping through the vertical blinds is what woke Reign. She sat up and looked around with her sleepy eyes. M was gone. He left her a note instructing her to let herself out. He had to go to the gym and run errands and didn't want to wake her.

This was the perfect time for her to make a move. She slid out of the bed and tiptoed around to the other side of the room. She cracked the door slowly to give an ear to the halls to verify if she was alone. She wasn't sure, but she seemed to be. She closed the door back and made her way over by the window opposite the round king bed where a desk sat overlooking the view of the deck.

Reign nervously peeked out the window to ensure she wasn't being watched. She sat at the desk and opened the top drawer. She rambled through it and found a picture of M and Token. It stopped her in her tracks. She stared at it for a minute, reminiscing of that night in Vegas. She threw the picture aside and continued to search.

Finding nothing in the top draw, she moved on to the second. This drawer was like the first, except it had more pictures of M and other women. None of them were of her or her sister. She didn't care. She just moved on to draw number three. Bingo. M had all his banking information in this drawer from what appeared to be his banker and blank checks. Reign kindly took out everything she needed, gently placing the remaining items back where she found them, making them appear to be untouched.

At this point, Reign tipped back over to the side of the bed she slept on, slid back into her worn clothing, tucked the banking papers in her bag, and saw herself out.

Chapter: 11

Chasity walked into the bank early today to attend a mandatory meeting. She had well anticipated the meeting. "Good morning, everyone. My name is Detective Bill Walls, and today, I'm here to educate everyone about counterfeit money. Some cities in Florida have set up a special task force for this problem, but here in Orlando, we haven't seen much of this, and one reason is that I, along with six other detectives, educate staff such as yourselves on how to detect and report this problem. You guys are our first line of defense. How? I'll tell you how. Once the counterfeiters begin to produce the millions of bills, the first thing they do is try to switch them out at banks. This is why you guys have to understand the nature and terminology of these perpetrators."

The room grew still as everyone held on to their brown metal chairs. To some, this was one of the most critical events in their lives. They felt they had a purpose. Chasity felt the same, but she didn't feel like she was a part of that team. She had her on the team. And with that, she jotted all the notes down on her iPad and waited patiently for this class to end.

The detective went on about paper type, even giving them a sample to feel. He went from one extreme to the next about these counterfeit bills without knowing who was in attendance. The class finally ended, and Chas raced home to share the knowledge with Reign.

By Wednesday evening, Fed-Ex had been dropping off everything from cleaning supplies to cartons and ink, paper, Windex, Easy Off, rope, clothes pins, and Armor Oil. These were just a few of the essentials for the operation to succeed.

They had turned the guest room into a production room. Reign laid out six Pyrex dishes on a rectangular folding table and began to pour. Each dish held its contents to be used in order. While Reign set up the lab, Chas hung a rope from one end of the room to the other. The desk with the Mac computer sat nearby, making it easy for Reign and Chas to jump from one task to another.

"You know, I forgot to tell you we needed blank checks as well," Chas spoke in Reign's direction.

"Got them," Reign swiftly answered back.

"What about the account numbers? I have a couple, but we need someone with never-ending cash." Chasity laughed.

"Got that, too." Reign never looked up. She was in deep concentration as she tried to make the best 100-dollar bill outside the U.S. Bureau of Engraving and Printing.

As the laser light flashed, producing the image, Reign turned that one bill too many in seconds with a click of the mouse. Through minutes of pure concentration, Reign could complete the most perfect bills. The bills were now wet. They carefully hung them on the rope and waited patiently for them to dry.

Reign could hear the phone ringing in the other room. She excused herself and went to answer it. While waiting, Chas jumped on the computer to create a business account in the company name Reign had registered. This was too easy for them.

Chasity sat at the computer thinking, Imagine having $100,000 at the snap of a finger without the risk of going in and out of banks. Although her imagination was taking over, she knew they were getting close. Reign talked a little longer, with the call more regular than usual. Therefore, Chas went to see what was holding her.

As she approached the kitchen, she could hear Reign pleading with Token for her forgiveness. Chas rolled her eyes and entered the kitchen to encourage Reign to hang up on TK. Before she could speak, Reign handed Chas the phone so she could have a word with her.

Reign walked away to dry her face. Chas took the phone geared up to let Token have it, but somehow, the tables turned quickly. Token was on the other end of the telephone, manipulating the shit out of Chas. She made Chas feel like she was the scum of the earth who had abandoned Token in her time of need. Chas didn't see this coming. She thought she was utterly controlling the conversation, but somehow it flipped. Now, she was crying as well.

The 15-minute phone call ended, and the girls returned to the room. "What did she say to you?" Chasity asked Reign, who was examining.

"Probably the same thing she said to you," Reign answered.

"So, how do you feel about it?" Chas asked. Reign shrugged her shoulders and walked to the window. "In one sense, I feel she's right, but in another, I feel you're right. I don't know what to think. But I know one thing. She isn't hungry anymore." They both laughed.

"Yeah, she'll be okay. We should have her back." Reign agreed as both ladies walked back over to finish examining the bills. They looked closely at the bills with a magnifying glass, looking for that one flaw that could cause their cover to be blown. They went up and down, looking at everything, including the red and blue fine printer hair on the bills, just like the authentic ones.

After carefully reviewing the bills, Chas turned to Reign. "Reign," she called slowly, "WE DID IT!" Both girls jumped for joy as they grabbed each other.

"There's no stopping us now. We got the grove," Reign sang from her lungs. They were both so happy. "Hey, you think The Department of Corrections would take it?"

"Probably not," they said in unison. They both fell on the floor laughing.

CHAPTER: 12

Early the following day, Reign was woken up by the house phone ringing. "Hello?"

"Hello, you have a collect call from Token Davis, an Inmate at the Florida Department of Corrections federal institute. Press one to accept and two to decline. (Beep) Thank you. You will not be billed for this call."

"Hello, Reign. Thank God. I have been thinking all night. I need you guys to do me a huge favor."

"What's that TK?" Token spoke as if she had forgotten about cursing Reign and Chas out on the previous phone call.

"How's your credit?"

"Credit?" Reign almost forgot the code they had spoken of a while back. Oh, that credit. It came back to her remembrance. "Yes, not only is it good, but it increased." She paused. "By a lot."

"That's what's up. Well, you guys have to do this for me."

"What is it TK?" By now, Reign was sitting in bed anxiously waiting for Token to spit out the favor.

"Sis, I need a lawyer."

"A lawyer? You have another case?" Reign was confused.

"No, big head. I want to file an appeal."

"What's an appeal?"

"Listen, I'll call you later. They are locking us down. Just call Mike and tell him what I said. He'll help."

The phone clicked, and the operator came on. "Your call has been terminated." Reign hit off on the cordless and lay there even more confused.

TOKEN: BACK ON IT

After hanging up the phone, Token returned to her bunk with a glee of hope. She was excited about Reign and Chas being on but still curious to know what they were doing. She wanted to be a part of it but knew it was impossible to do from there. Therefore, she waited patiently to hear more news from Reign. Since that last letter written home to the girls, Token decided she would be a little less fierce and more sentimental regarding her family and friends.

There were so many people she needed to apologize to, so many people she needed to face, but she wasn't sure how to. She didn't know where to start. Sitting there in deep thought, her bunkie interrupted her, sitting nearby at a medal desk that divided the two bunks.

"Sweetheart, don't worry about tomorrow. For tomorrow brings its worries. Today's trouble is enough."

That was Ms. June for you. She was always quoting the Good Book. I listened to her read and talk to herself a lot. She had three children, but they all abandoned her when she came to prison.

"Ms. June, can you give me your honest opinion?"

"Well, Sunshine, it depends."

"Depends on what." Token sat still, looking directly into Ms. June's face for an answer. "It depends on if you want an honest answer."

Token thought to herself, why would I ask for your honest opinion if I didn't want it? But she knew older people always had a way of spinning you.

"Yes, Ms. June. I want nothing but the truth. That's why I'm coming to you."

Ms. June turned around and carefully studied Token, remembering the day Token walked on that compound. She vividly recalled how Token sat pretty as if the world revolved around her. She watched daily as Token ate anything her heart desired, not offering her a crumb. There were plenty of nights she watched as Token tossed and turned in her sleep, fighting off her many demons. She never said a word. She just watched and prayed that this day would come.

"Well, I'm listening, Davis." Ms. June closed the Bible she was reading to give Token her undivided attention.

Now that Ms. June was ready to listen, Token wasn't sure if she would open up. "Ms. June, what would you do if you had a friend who was a good friend to you, but you were a bad friend to them, and they needed your help now?"

"Well, I guess the question would be, can you help? Furthermore, did you ever make amends with that friend?" Token remained attentive as Ms. June began to school her friendships. She spoke of a friendship of 30 years that ended with her best friend dying of breast cancer, and she never got to say goodbye. She never had a chance to amend those broken fences. Those words alone led to an hour-long conversation interrupted by count time.

As Token sat up straight like a soldier while the C.O.s came through counting, she thought of Ms. June's words. It was true. She needed to reach out to her childhood friend and make amends no matter what it took. When the count cleared, Token jumped at the chance to get out paper and pen to get writing.

She was excited about the courage Ms. June gave her to reach out to her friend. She thought long and hard about what she would say but knew she had to start somewhere. As she propped the pillow underneath her head, she took out her purple pen and began to write:

Dear Cheeks, I know you're wondering why it took this long to write, or maybe you're even wondering why I'm writing to you. Well, the truth is, I wanted to apologize for everything that has happened over the years. I'm sorry.

Token balled up the paper but was unable to continue. She wanted to reach out but was scared Cheeks wouldn't accept her apology. She didn't want to take the blame for everything. Although she knew many of her influences played a vital role in Cheek's life, she still felt it wasn't 100 percent her fault and wasn't ready to take the blame.

"CHOW!" the C.O. yelled from the bubble. It was a perfect time to shower while the other inmates rushed to the chow hall.

CHAPTER: 13

Token had given Reign the name of a reputable attorney in Miami. Reign knew very little about what Token was speaking of. She called this attorney but had to leave a message. She was happy to have Token back in her good graces. She wanted her to depend on her. She was astatic that her sister trusted her to make things happen. Things were looking up for all three of them.

Chasity had Mr. Witterman's head so far in the clouds. He had no time to investigate any of her wrongdoings. She stayed on top of the know in the office. She would have known if there was any buzz about counterfeit money. Chasity emailed Detective Bill regularly. Most of it was small talk, but she used that time to focus on counterfeit money and see if anything new was happening.

She picked him regularly without raising suspicion. She used that time to flirt to get the answers.

The name Mona Blackman rang bells on the southeast end. She was a prominent lawyer. She was the new female version of the late great Johnnie Cochran. Token had given Reign the task of calling and getting her on the team. Token said it would cost a pretty penny, but Reign didn't care. She was determined to do whatever it took to remain in Token's good graces.

Reign picked up the phone to place a call to Ms. Blackman. It wasn't long before Reign and Chas were in South Beach bond. The two couldn't wait to turn this business trip into an adventure. She and Chas didn't pack anything but the pups to take to the doggie daycare.

The girls made it to Miami safely. She was ready for the consultation with Ms. Blackman but Not before taking in the new surroundings. Reign had been in Florida for some time, but this would be the first time South Beach would be there. With no knowledge of the infamous town, she was forced to use a travel agent to book them in the two-bedroom penthouse suite at the Intercontinental. The shit was sweet, but the girls had no time to waste sitting around a hotel; they had shopping to do. They dropped their bags off and hit Aventura Mall in seconds.

When they hit the lobby, they didn't hesitate to have the concierge call them for a cab. But they couldn't have an ordinary cab; they needed a luxury one. It wasn't long before the white Cadillac Escalade pulled up along the roundabout to pick the ladies up.

Reign darted for the door handle when Chas abruptly stopped her. "Chill, Re. We have to let the help." 'Help,' she winked as they both watched a short and stocky man with a Spanish accent make his way around the car to open the door for the both of them.

They stepped into the car one after the other, laughing at Chas's comments. They both took their seats, one at each window, admiring the sights. "Man, Token would have loved this," Reign said quietly but loud enough for Chasity to hear. Chas didn't respond; she just sat back, wondering why Reign always felt guilty for living her life.

Why could Token live without regrets, but Reign was full of them? Maybe being an only child had something to do with it, but for her life, she couldn't and didn't understand it. They pulled up to the Aventura Mall quickly as hell. They never had time to exchange words about the trip.

They both were in their zones. Reign indeed missed her sister and wanted to do everything she could for her, but she slowly but surely realized what life was about on her own. She no longer felt like a slave to Token's rhythm. It was Chasity and Token who were oblivious to this fact. Reign, on the other hand, knew exactly what she was doing, Or at least, that's what she thought.

"First up, the Gucci Store," Reign announced as they entered the mall entrance.

"Since when did you start liking Gucci?" Chas raised a brow.

"Oh, it's not that I love Gucci. It's Gucci who loves us." Reign retorted.

Chas didn't say another word. She just watched Reign slowly changing into someone else she wasn't ready for, someone else being TOKEN.

"Look, Chas!" Reign shouted excitedly as she sashayed across the floor, picking up numerous big-ticket items. Chas was anxious to shop, too. But was more concerned about the counterfeit bills they had on them. Chas remembered what the detective said in their very first meeting. She went home that day and ran down everything to Reign word by word, but Reign thought she was above it all for some reason. They hadn't been in the store for over twenty minutes, and Reign had piled more than $10,000 of merchandise on the counter.

Chas wanted to add some things but paid close attention to the well-dressed security guards in the store.

"Chas, I thought you wanted that new Hobo bag over there in white." Chas admired the bag, but something about these two gentlemen changed her mind.

"I'm gonna walk outside to take this call." Chas raised her cell phone as if it was a real call coming through. She then walked out of the store and over to the food court, where she could continue to get a good view of the store.

Chas wasn't sure if she wanted to be involved in this venture anymore. Going out of town and passing fake bills was not part of her plans. Although she loved nice things, the more she thought about trading places with Token, the more shaken she became. She didn't mind playing her part at the bank. She had her way of staying in the know, which gave her peace of mind.

Chas watched from a distance as Reign pretended to be on the phone. She cringed as she witnessed Reign pull out several bills and hand them to the sales clerk. Reign stood at the counter, impatiently tapping her foot for the sales team to hurry. After five minutes of waiting, they finally released the goods to her, and she headed out of the store like a faithful shopper.

When Reign reached Chas, she considered herself to be in the clear. As she grew closer to her, she could hear her finishing up a conversation with Mr. Witterman.

Reign walked up and instantly checked Chas. "So, did you need to take that phone call ?" She gave Chas a sarcastic look.

Chas swore up and down that it was a critical business call and needed to get back to the hotel pronto to continue. Reign was pissed, and she had no clue as to why Chas did what she did.

The woman exited the building to head to their hired car, which waited nearby. They didn't say much on the ride back. Instead, Reign concentrated on her new items.

Just then, she handed Chas a bag with a smile. "You didn't think I would forget about you, did you?

Chas smiled as she lifted the Winter White Gucci Hobo purse from the shopping bag. "You a mess, lil sis. But I love you." She reached across the seat to give Reign a big hug. The driver swiftly returned to the hotel, and the girls headed in to grab a bite to eat and take a nap before checking out the nightlife.

CHAPTER: 14

Token's days were pretty much determined for her. She was told when to eat, sleep, wash, speak, and break for free. Today was no different from the others. Except there was a detail assigned to Token, and she had no idea until she heard her name being called from the officer's bubble. "Are you Ms. Davis?"

Token took off her inmate ID, which hung from the pocket of her uniform, and put it to the window to confirm.

The C.O. then Popped the steel door to let her out. She walked out of the dorm and along the white lines designed for the inmate's movement. It was 4:00 pm, and the yard was closed for the next hour. Token had never traveled alone on the compound. It was usually with her unit, but today was different. She was called out to report to the kitchen. She had been selected for work detail. Unhappy, she entered the kitchen manager's office and waited for further instructions.

She lined up on the wall where other inmates were waiting for their uniforms. Token thought this was crazy. She knew for sure she'd be able to at least pick where she would slave. But boy, was she wrong.

The three chicks ahead of her seemed to have been excited. They gave each other high fives and talked about how they would be hooking their people up.

It was wild. Token stayed as far away from the Chow hall as she could, so to be working in it was a push. Finally, the heavyset, overweight black man called her last name. She was the last to be seen and couldn't wait to get it over with.

Word on the street was that this manager guy was a creep. He prayed on the captivated woman, quickly sized her up, and issued two white uniforms and a pair of work boots. Token looked at the entire outfit with disgust while the other inmates walked away smiling and boasting as if they had scored the newest Timberlands.

When the manager dismissed her, she was eager to return to the dorm to call Reign to find out what happened with the lawyer. She made her way to the breezeway, and that's as far as she got before she heard someone yelling across the compound, referring to her as just plain Inmate. At first, Token neglected to stop because she knew he couldn't possibly be talking to her. He called again, "INMATE!"

Token turned and looked in his direction. Looking around, she realized no other inmate was out in the courtyard; therefore, he had to be talking to her. He waved at her to come to him. She needed clarification. She knew the yard wasn't open, and it was almost time for count. Why would the Sergent be calling her? Did he need to tell her something about her case? Token was puzzled but made a U-turn back in his direction. "Yes, Sarge." Token looked in the sergeant's face. It wasn't until she realized how sexy this sergeant was. He was spoken of frequently on the compound but never anything good. She thought every woman who laid their eyes on him hated him.

Serge took his time examining Token. Although she appeared a little rough, he could tell she had to be a force to be reckoned with on those streets. Today wasn't a first for him. He'd been watching her. He was on classification duty the day the bus pulled in and she got off. He watched as she made her way through, trying her best not to stand out from the other female inmates. He did his research. He didn't ask around about her, but he didn't hesitate to run to the computer and look up her case.

From how the courts spoke of her and her criminal activities, he knew she was about that life. It excited him. It wasn't every day that he would see someone truly about it and not boasting in the yard about it. It was more like she was ashamed and wanted no part of her reputation.

"What's your name?" He asked as if he didn't know. Not only did he know her name, but he also knew where she was from, where she was next to kin, and her blood type.

"It's Token," she answered before correcting herself.

"Sorry, sir. It's Davis.

"Davis? Ms. Davis, where are you coming from? He continued as if he didn't know. In all actuality, he was the one who had her put on kitchen duty. He needed to get her out of that dorm so he could make his move. It was hard to prey on someone who always stayed on her bunk. She would only step out for the canteen or if instructed.

Token thought about her answer. She had no choice but to tell the truth, but she wasn't sure whether she was in trouble.

"The kitchen, sir." She stood straight up like a soldier determined to be obedient.

The sergeant studied her again. Although her jacket said one thing to him, he couldn't see it. He didn't know that person the courts spoke of. What he saw was surprising to him. He saw a beautiful woman that somehow got fucked up in this world. As they stood there face-to-face, he had no more words to say.

His radio was going off, and it was officially time for count. "It's count time, and this yard is closed. It would be best if you were not walking around. Let me escort you back to your dorm. "What dorm are you in?"

Another question he knew the answer to.

"B dorm, sir."

He called into the radio to escort an inmate to dorm B. When they reached the door, he pulled out his key and opened it.

"Inmate, go straight to your bunk and get ready for count."

"Yes, sir." Token turned and walked into the dorm, where all the ladies were quiet and waiting to be counted.

CHAPTER: 15

Reign and Chas came to Miami ready for this night. They had yet to see the lawyer but fulfilled just about everything else they wanted to. While relaxing at the pool earlier, they were given a couple of VIP passes to a club on the strip.

They were told it was the hot spot in Miami. Not knowing much about the Big City, the name Liv didn't mean much to them. The two women dressed, beating each other to the one-wall mirror to admire herself.

Chas looked great in her shoulder-out, long-length, black fitted dress with a split from her ankle to her upper thigh area. But the black and gold Christian Louboutin shoes she had chosen stood out more than anything. She knew she looked good and couldn't wait to get into the club to meet new money.

It was a bit more challenging when it was Reign's turn to give herself the final approval. Reign had the classy dress in the bag, but the sexiness was not so much. It took Chas's work to swoop her hair up in a chignon hairdo that complemented the red Gucci mini-skirt and halter.

To Reign, it did not do much for her shape, but Chas reassured her that her ensemble was a sure-nuff show-stopper. Once the two agreed with their reflections, they headed out the door to meet the driver again.

The club appeared to be crowded. The line was around the corner. They passed by many patrons waiting to get in. "Reign, look!" Chas pointed out her window. That looks like Baby from Cash Money." Reign looked but wasn't impressed. She felt she had money, just like he did. Hers may not have been confirmed, but it was hers.

Besides this was South Beach, the home of the *Every Notes*.?

"You see him?" Chas asked again in a groupie tone.

"Look, I'm not doing all that, and besides, that's not him anyway."

The driver finally made a stop to let them out. The tall, muscular male who was very well dressed directed the traffic. "Good evening, ladies. Are you on the VIP List? Chas scrambles through her purse, looking for the VIP passes given to them earlier.

"Yes, we are P-A-S-H-I?"

"It's Pashi," The man uttered, feeling disrespected.

"Yeah, whatever," Reign laughed, tapping him on his back simultaneously, but Pashi didn't find anything amusing about what she said. He hurried his eyes down the iPod, looking for their names to be listed. "What did you say the names listed were?"

Chas responded, "Chasity and Reign."

"As in, make it Reign." Reign interjected, giving a glance at the fake hundreds.

Either way, he let them in because he'd wasted enough time with these two and needed to return to his job. Once in, the girls strolled into The VIP entrance, passing security and into a small booth. The party was banging. It's no wonder why this is the livest place on the beachside. The two were head turners, and they knew it. Everyone was trying to get a glimpse of them. A barmaid finally made it over to get their drink orders. They ordered a little of everything. They figured it was a club and would never check the bills.

The music was pumping, and Reign was putting on all the latest dance moves. She knew how to dance; Chas, on the other hand, was not doing so well. But that soon changed after a couple of the mixed concoctions; Chas had stepped her two-step game up.

Vibing to sounds that blasted out the speakers, the two stopped in their tracks, their hands still in the air, and the other held their drink. They were baffled when the DJ announced the Orlando basketball team was in the building. Instead, they both were ready to blow the joint. Reign more so than Chas. This would be Reign's first time coming face to face with L while in the presence of Chas. How would she act? What would she say? Would he act normal or hint at the fact that they messed around to make Chas jealous?

She didn't know what to expect. All she knew was that she would try to stay out of his view. "I'm about to use the restroom," Reign told Chas as she hurried about, hoping Chas got the hint and didn't want to follow.

"Ok, I'll stay here and nurse these drinks."

Glad to hear Chas wouldn't follow, Reign went to the bathroom, where she stopped and took a deep breath. On her way, she peeked around to see if she had seen L, but so far, she had not. And just because his team was there didn't mean he was there, too.

In the restroom, Reign overheard a woman talking about the rappers and ball players in the building tonight. She didn't hear L's name but overheard them exchanging stories about Lil Wayne. This was crazy, she thought to herself. These chicks think it's a badge of honor to fuck this little ass dude. She shook her head while she washed her hands.

Reign was then eager to get back out there with Chas. She accepted the towel from the bathroom bitch, then made her way back to where she and Chas sat. When she got back, she was taken by surprise. Chas was still there, but she had company. Jason somehow found her, and Reign wasn't excited about it. "Hey, how are you, mum?" L snapped his finger as if he had no clue who she was.

"Reign, silly." Chas playfully shoved L. Reign was baffled once again. She didn't know how to take L's unexpected behavior. On the one hand, she was glad he didn't put their business on blast, but he made her feel used on the other.

Reign finally got up enough courage to speak back.

"Hey, Jason," she said, waving him off and then walking over to the other side of the booth, where she would be out of their faces. Reign poured herself a glass and tried her hardest not to look in their direction.

The night was still pretty young, and Reign took advantage of it. While L and Chas stayed in the VIP area catching up on lost times, Reign took to the dance floor and got her groove on.

The DJ started playing old-school jams. Although Reign was too young to remember the old-school artists, the vibe was still young. She was a dancer, so catching on to the old-school dances was easy. She danced until the last call for alcohol. Her feet were killing her. Reign made her way over to an open booth and took a seat.

She pulled out her cell phone to call Chas and let her know she was ready to go. Chas's phone went to voicemail. Reign decided to text instead: Hey, I'm ready to go. Where are you? She pushed send and waited for a reply.

Chas texted back: I'll meet you back at the hotel, and I'm going to chill with L Ttyl.

Reign just put her head down on the table. She couldn't believe Chas was falling for L again. She texted her again: *Are you serious? You're going to go with that loser? This Nigga played you and left you to starve smh.* She waited again, but this time, there was no response.

It was then that Reign realized she was alone. She called the driver and made her way out to the front to be picked up. She jumped in the truck and pulled out her phone again to give Chas a piece of her mind, but she decided against it. The driver pulled up in front of the hotel, and Reign waited for him to open the door. Then, she handed him a fifty—a real one. He thanked her, and he disappeared out of sight.

CHAPTER: 16

The sun beamed through the blinds, waking Reign. She rolled over and looked at the time. It was after 9:00 AM. "OMG!" Reign jumped out of bed and searched for her phone to call Ms. Blackman. Her receptionist answered and took the message that she would be late. Reign damn near tripped over her own two feet as she hurried to jump in the shower.

Not putting in much effort, Reign brushed the strands of her hair back in the bun, threw on her sweat suit, and flew out the door. When she made it downstairs, the driver had just pulled up. Reign was relieved. She didn't want to blow this for her sister.

The driver asked where to go, and she gave him the law firm's name in Biscayne. As they rode over the Causeway bridge, Reign couldn't help but examine her phone to see if she'd missed any calls from Chas. She didn't. She rode in complete silence and thought about the events from last night. She couldn't believe how L acted as he was not interested.

She wanted to burst his bubble but didn't want to alarm Chasity. The driver finally pulled up to Ms. Blackman's firm's building. Reign exited the car but asked the driver to wait for her. It wasn't until her feet pounded the majestic marble and granite floors that she knew this would cost a pretty penny.

She walked to the elevator and looked at the stone directory on the wall to place Ms. Blackman's name. She then spotted her name and followed the numbers until she reached her office. "Reign Davis here to see Ms. Blackman."

Reign didn't wait for an intro. She walked up to the cherry wood oval desk and announced herself. The slender black woman seated behind it reminded her of a younger version of the English model Naomi Campbell. She was charming and wasn't moved by Reign's arrogance. The woman looked up and then back downward at the computer, looking for Reign's appointed time.

When she found the slot, she realized Reign was tardy, and that was a no-no on Ms. Blackman's watch. "Ms. Davis," the woman called out. Reign turned her focus back to the woman. "Yes."

"Ms. Davis, your appointment with Ms. Blackman was well over an hour ago, and Ms. Blackman is a stickler who is on time.

"I know. I know. Can you tell her that I'm not from here and that I got lost? I will pay an extra five thousand if need be. I need to see her today. Please, ma'am." Those words fell off her lips so quickly that she didn't give it any thought. Chasity had prepared authentic certified bank checks to cover the fees. She didn't have any extra on her that was legit, but she figured if she could get in there to her, she'd figure the rest out later. Besides, she called to let them know she'd be a little late. That should count for something. Reign thought to herself.

The woman picked up the phone and could be heard relaying the message. I'm unsure of the response, but Reign kept a close ear, praying that Ms.Blackman would understand. The woman hung up the phone and instructed Reign to have a seat.

Two hours had passed, and Reign grew impatient. She kept pacing the floor, trying to gain the woman's attention, hoping it would prompt her to call Ms. Blackman again. It didn't. It wasn't until after one o'clock that she was called into Ms. Blackman's office.

When Reign walked in, she was taken aback by the lavish décor. The walls looked as if they were hand-crafted with deep designs symbolizing freedom of some sort. The colors chosen made one feel revived. Reign was impressed. She wasn't sure what the inside of a law firm looked like, but she was sure this was far from the norm.

Reign waited inside the waiting area of Ms. Blackman's office. She thought she would get to the consultation once she made it inside, but she was wrong. It was another twenty minutes before Ms. Blackman finally opened the door adjacent to the office she waited in. Ms. Blackman stood six feet tall with long jet-black hair and beautiful big brown eyes. She was breathtaking. The women in this firm should be on magazine covers. They were the epitome of *America's Top Models.* "Hello, Ms. Davis. My name is Mona Blackman. Please have a seat."

Reign was mesmerized by her poise and good deportment. Reign complied. Ms. Blackman sat behind her glass desk and looked up Token's case. She started speaking about it, and Reign listened to it while enjoying the view of the Biscayne Bay from the office wall's window.

Ms. Blackman spoke too many legal terms, including appeals, motions, litigation, and other things that pertained to Token's case. Reign was clueless. She had the slightest idea of what this lady was talking about. All she wanted to know was how much and how long.

CHAPTER: 17

Chasity woke up with a banging headache. She looked around the room, trying to remember where she was. She rolled over in the king-size bed right into L's lips.

He sheepishly kissed her back. Chas couldn't resist the hold L had on her. She was hooked on the money and all that good hardcore sex. She didn't know how she could ever be with anyone else. L had her heart, her soul, and her mind. She would do anything for him. Even if it meant being with a couple of his teammates.

As she kissed L passionately, she remembered vaguely last night's episodes. She remembered getting to the hotel room and having more to drink. She remembered the room being full of naked women and men. When she walked through the door, she thought, by far, this would not be something that she and L would be a part of. She knew he would never want to share her, just like she would never want to share him. Not amused by any activities, Chasity made a beeline straight for the main suite and undressed, wanting for L. But to her surprise, she came walking another 7-foot male that she had seen before but wasn't sure of his name. He began to kiss her without an invitation. She tried to resist, but in walked L with two more partners.

He instructed her to get on all fours and take turns giving each player ahead. She was hesitant and nervous initially, but it wasn't until L said, "If you loved me, you'd do it.

" That eased her mind." She loved him and hoped to be back in the house with him soon, and if this was what it took to prove her loyalty, then she was all in.

The sex has to have lasted all night. The guys took turns ramming their dicks into her as if she had no walls. Some were bigger than others, causing her to let out screams at times, turning the guys on even more. What she thought should have felt good didn't feel good. It was the worst feeling she had ever felt.

Lying there kissing L now formed a bit of solace. "Slow down," L told her as he turned his body away from Chas.

"Huh?" Chas was confused. She was ready to play along, and L turned his back to her. Not ready to give up, she put her tits on his back and began stroking his manhood from behind.

"STOP!" L rejected her for the third time. Chas wasn't going to stay around and get dismissed again. With that being said, she stood to her feet and got dressed. Tears slowly streamed out of her eyes as she watched L nonchalantly lay there as if he had no feelings for her at all.

She wanted to ask him questions but figured it would further complicate things, so she would instead leave it be. When fully dressed, she walked to the door, ready to exit, when L stopped her. "Chas!" he yelled out in a muffled tone.

He does care, " Chas thought to herself and smiled. She turned around, ready to return to his arms and accept his apology.

"Close the door behind you." Chas's heart fell. *This asshole!* It was the most she could say as she made her way out of the room and down to the lobby, where she called Reign, hoping she wasn't too mad and would send the driver to pick her up.

Reign exited Ms. Blackman's office feeling hopeful. Ms. Blackman didn't make any promises but had a powerful sense of hope. Reign may not have understood everything, but the word possibility was good enough for her. The driver caught a glimpse of Reign before she made it out from behind the revolving glass doors and prepared for her entrance to the SUV.

"Good day, Ms. Davis. Are we headed back to the hotel?"

"Yes, please." The driver closed the door, and Reign was comfortable in the back seat. She rested her head back, closed her eyes, thinking about the possibility of her sister being freed, and smiled. Her thoughts were interrupted by the unique sound of her text tone from Chas.

She wanted to be picked up from L's hotel room. Reign didn't have a problem picking her up, but with L's money, why didn't he have his driver drop her off? He was the one who took her there. This wasn't the time for the third-degree; besides, Chas wasn't there to hear her vent anyway, so she gave the address to the driver, and they headed to the hotel to pick her up.

Chas quickly jumped in the Cadillac like she was running from the police or something. Reign looked astonished by this behavior. "What the fuck Chas? Don't tell me you got into it with one of his little tramps."

"No," Chas answered, all annoyed. "Can you tell the driver to hit it, please?" Chas begged. Reign looked to the front and gave the man a head node, and he continued on the journey.

The ride started silent, but Reign refused to miss the opportunity to hear about L. She needed to know what happened between those two that caused Ms. Hottie to be back on the ride with her after she totally abandoned her and didn't even make it to the lawyer's office to see about Token. "Well, let's hear it." Reign turned in Chasity's direction, waiting for the story to begin.

"Let's hear what?" Chas snapped back. "Don't act stupid; you know what I'm talking about. What happened with King L?"

"Look, Reign, I'm not in the mood for you to play, Mommy Dearest. What happened between L and me isn't anyone's business. I think I'm grown enough to handle my own."

Reign laughed. "Then, why the fuck I'm I here picking you up? Your grown ass should have called a cab, or your balling boyfriend should have sent you home with a driver." Reign was ready to curse Chasity's ass out. She was tired of her. She stopped where she was and didn't go any further because she knew if she started, she would get her for the old and the new. Chas sat tapping her foot, dying for the driver to hurry to their destination.

She wanted nothing more than to be alone with her hurt feelings. Reign looked over at Chas from the corner of her eyes and witnessed the tears flowing from her eyes. She couldn't help but wonder if L had told her about them. It was killing her inside that she didn't know. She figured she'd pick and pick until Chasity broke.

The driver finally made his way into the roundabout at the hotel. Neither one of them waited for the Driver to open the door. They both hopped out and made their way toward the entrance, damn near knocking people over to get to the elevator.

Chas looked at herself in the glass mirror, trying to fix her messy hair. Reign just watched as she thought of the words she would say once they entered the room. The bell rang, and the elevator door opened. Reign slowed as she dug deep in her Gucci purse for the key.

Chas had one, too, but from the looks of things, she either lost it or wasn't in any rush to get in the room. They reached the door, and Reign opened it. The girls walked in one after another, headed in the same direction.

Reign headed to the living area, and Chas headed past it to go directly to her room. "I sure hope L invited you back to live with him because your time is up with me and my sister."

Chasity stopped in her tracks. She didn't want to argue, but Reign pushed her far past the limit. "Listen, you little ungrateful bitch, I am so sick and tired of you acting like you and your sister was my saving grace! I knew how to hustle before you all came along, and I'll be fine when you bounce!"

Was that it? Was that all she was going to say.? *Why the hell isn't she saying what L told her about her*? Reign thought. Why wasn't she screaming at her for sleeping with L? Reign figured she'd try a different approach to get Chas to talk. "Y'all mixed breeds swear you all got everything under control! You all swear you can have anyone in any way you like, but I have news for you. You can't! And don't think I haven't heard all the shit you be talking about me and my sister!"

Reign studied Chasity's look on her face. It was a little confusing because Chas looked confused, which made Reign even more confused. This was becoming a hassle for Reign. She wasn't good at this particular activity and didn't know how to trick people into telling her what she wanted to hear.

"LISTEN, I'VE TAKEN ENOUGH ABUSE FROM PEOPLE, AND I AM TIRED! NOW, I HAVE NEVER SAID A WORD ABOUT YOU OR YOUR SISTER OUTSIDE THE PRESENCE OF THE TWO

OF US. YOU PRANCE YOUR ASS AROUND HERE AS IF YOU DID SOMETHING BIG. REIGN, I DID THIS SHIT! I PUT MY FREEDOM ON THE LINE. I LOVE TOKEN. ALTHOUGH I THINK SHE PUT WAY TOO MUCH PRESSURE ON YOU. I LOVE HER. BUT I LOVE YOU MORE!"

Reign stood there stunned. She wanted to pick Chas, not hurt her. It was all starting to backfire on Her. She was losing her pose. Chasity had yet to mention that Reign slept with L. Maybe she didn't know. Maybe L didn't open his mouth. If he didn't, that was thoughtful of him, she thought. Or perhaps he was holding this secret like a trump card. Whatever the reason was, Reign was beginning to feel guilty about doing what she did.

It was eating her up inside, and she could only pray that it would never come to the surface. "I'm Sorry, Chas. I never meant to hurt your feelings. Please stop crying. We will get past this."

"I know. I feel like every time you get upset, you say I'm using you and TK. Why do you keep saying that? How can I prove my loyalty? I have nothing but love for you two, but I'm tired Reign. I'm tired of not knowing where I belong." Chas sniffled in between words.

Reign had little to say. She opened a Kleenex box and began wiping Chas's face. The two had a bond, whether or not they wanted to admit it. They were bonded by theft, lies, and sex ties. At that moment, the girls put their differences aside and hugged one another. They began by chatting about the separate dates. Reign told her about the good news concerning Token, and they both began celebrating until it was time to check out in the morning.

CHAPTER: 18

"You look great, TK," Chasity said as they hugged briefly before the C.O. rudely reproved her. Chasity stepped aside to give Reign the room to embrace her older sister.

Token had made a tremendous turnaround from the last visit. She had relaxed and cut her natural jet-black mane into an excellent style. She had her bangs trimmed to lay flat across her forehead, and she left the length long with light layers that hung past her shoulders. The blue scrub-like uniform that she wore was crisp and creased. Her pants fell nicely on top of her sparkling white leather Nikes.

Token's face was even cleared of the pimples that once occupied too much damn space. "Yeah, TK. You look incredible for prison." The three ladies sat at the table, ready to enjoy the six-hour visit. Reign spent much of the visit assuring Token she had everything under control. Both ladies pretended not to see the long scar on Token's face, which she had received years prior in county jail.

Although Token was pleased with her little sister's progress, she knew she had created a monster. The last thing she wanted was for her little sister to trade places with her. She watched as Reign switched around the visitation room, begging for attention from the men in uniform. Like a true baller, she walked back and forth to the canteen window to purchase more food, and money was no option.

Token scoped out the diamond bracelet Reign wore and knew it cost over five G's just from its looks. From the time Reign landed in Florida until now, Reign had lost every bit of 15 pounds, transforming her body to a perfect 10. She only stood about five feet four inches and weighed around 145 pounds. She was wearing the hell out of her Dolce and Gabanna jeans.

Their presence alone was ringing bells in the hall. They had gotten up to take pictures, and all eyes were on them. They got over the props and were clowning the entire time. They struck poses like they were Charlie's Angels. Everyone watched as the girls had a fantastic time together. They were happy they could put a smile on Token's face. She'd been down for a little while now, but it wouldn't be long before she'd hit the bricks again, and O-Town was not ready for these three.

Later that evening, Chas and Reign made it home from the visit with just enough time to go back to the lab and print more bills. They have been spending and not saving an ounce for the last two months. They were on a roll, and no one was onto them for now.

Chas got too sleepy to finish and called it a night.

Reign was persistent. She would stay up all night if that's what it took. But with staying up comes boredom, which started to set in. As she waited for the bills to print, Reign picked up her phone and secretly began texting M. She said just a few words, testing him to see if he would text back.

She was afraid of the response if he did decide to text her back. She waited almost twenty minutes before he finally hit her back: "***Well, hello, beautiful.***" The text read.

Was this dude just stupid or plain slow? Did he not know that over seventy g's were missing from his account? Reign didn't physically take the money out of his account, but with the numbers on the bottom of his checks and Chas contacting his banker, this looks like a legitimate withdrawal.

She finally regained his attention and wanted to ensure she didn't lose it again: **"Hey,** *Sweetheart, how have you been?* Reign had nothing but time to waste, and what better way to do it than with a man with money?

I've been thinking about you lately…..

Oh yeah, how much? Enough to make me come over tonight……

(lol)Not tonight, sweetie. I'm busy preparing for a fight, but I would love to see you soon…..

OK, just let me know ……

I will ttyl……

kool ttyl.

Reign felt relieved knowing everything was ok with M. She needed to tell him Token would be coming home soon. She wouldn't have told him if she hadn't been so sure. But she was sure because Ms. Blackman found many flaws in the Token case, even down to how the evidence was handled. She said the state wanted her so badly that they would do anything to get her. Token had people from all over testifying about shit they heard, which made her case strictly precise, but they testified as if they had first-hand knowledge, which was illegal.

CHAPTER: 19

Reign waited patiently as she boarded her plane to Atlantic City. She packed light because this was only a one-day trip. She had nothing but a carry-on, making her travel easy to navigate in and out of the airports. She hadn't discussed with Chasity where she was going. That would only make her secret no longer a secret. Reign walked onto the plane and put her carry-on up in the overhead.

She sat in her seat with her head in the clouds. She wasn't sure why she accepted the invite when she knew what she was doing was wrong. But she wanted to do this in person. She needed to end this. Token was coming home soon, and Reign knew she had no room in this man's life. She figured if she needed to do this face to face, this was one of the most embarrassing things she had done. How could she take over where her sister left off?

Tight Mike Dickenson and L should have been off-limits. What was she thinking of? How could she do this to the only two people who loved her?

Chasity sat on the living room couch, bored as hell. She had no idea where Reign was and didn't want to be bothered by the older man, Witterman. She picked up her phone to call L. The phone rang and rang, but there was no answer. She started to leave a message but figured that was just a waste of time. She'd come to realize L only cared about himself. To Chasity, this was no way to live. Her parents disowned her the moment she decided she wasn't going to do what they wanted her to do. And she moved out to live with L. That was the icing on the cake.

She had no one. She had no real family, and everything she did and everyone she knew seemed to come with a motive. Nothing seemed sincere anymore.

Chas didn't want to use this time alone to soak in despair. Instead, she got up off of the couch and went into her room and popped on a porno, and enjoyed herself with a dildo she'd purchased not too long ago.

That session restored the smile on her face and made her feel like a new woman again. With that being said, she didn't need L to return her call, and she damn sure wasn't wanting the company of Mr. Witterman. She pleased herself, got up, took a long bath, and pinned her hair up for work the next day.

When Reign landed in Atlantic City, she strolled through the sea of people, contemplating whether or not she wanted to go through with this visit. There were so many butterflies hopping around in her stomach. Something was telling her to turn around and go back, but as she made her way through the airport, she saw nothing but posters of Mike reminding her of why this visit was necessary. She needed to end this before Token got home.

No one knew any actual dates, but they knew it was happening soon. Now was the time; she had to do this. As she exited the airport, many taxi drivers approached her, wanting to know where she would travel. She called Mike, and he instructed her to come to The Caesar's Palace, where he would have someone from his team meet her and pay the carfare. It didn't take long for her to arrive—at least, it only felt like a couple of minutes.

It had been a minute since Reign had been anywhere near Jersey City, and she felt the excitement in her belly. When she pulled up, they were waiting just as Mike said he would be. She opened the door and waited for directions from Mike's security team. Once the gentleman paid for the cab ride, he walked swiftly in front of Reign, leading her to the penthouse suite.

When she arrived, she expected a little more than just a greeting from Mike. She wanted more. She wanted the royal treatment he had given Token. Where was her red light special? This just wasn't her idea of a five-diamond date. Mike met her at the door with open arms. He smiled from ear to ear as he admired Reign's body in her outfit. He didn't know what she was wearing. He just knew it looked good on her.

On the other hand, Reign noticed how different Mike looked. He had to have lost at least 10 lbs. He didn't have a fresh cut, and the scruffy beard didn't do him justice. Reign tried hard to mask the expression on her face. *Was this the same damn man?* It was unbelievable what her eyes were witnessing. Don't just stand there. Make yourself comfortable." Mike spoke with a sluggish tone.

Reign walked around the suite to see if Mike was alone. Where was his trainer? Who was letting him do this to himself? As far as Reign could see, there wasn't a sign of anyone. But what she did find Opened her eyes a little wider to this harsh reality. There were drugs and booze Everywhere. " MIKE!" she called out, not realizing she sounded like someone's mother.

"Yes, baby." He walked into the room and looked at Reign, staring at the table. "Oh, I see you found the candy." He took a seat back in front of the drugs and picked up the plate it was on

And begin chopping it up in a fine pile.

Reign watched as he took a playing card, bent it, and pushed the white powder on it. And if that wasn't enough, he put the card to his nose and took a long, hard sniff, causing him to go backward in his chair. Shocking was an understatement. Reign didn't have a clue on what to do. So she did what she knew best. She ran into the other bedroom, locked the door, and cried. She was two hours away from her hometown and had no one to call. Token fucked all that up.

The City was mad at her, and Reign was guilty by association or relation. Either way, she was alone and scared.

Mike never bothered her. He let her sleep. He didn't want her to be worried. He just wanted to show her a good time, as he'd done many times. It was now three o'clock, and Reign was certain Mike had drunk and drugged himself to sleep. Although she was there because he invited her, she wasn't stupid. She had a plan—a plan that would make her trip worthwhile.

She opened the door slowly, listening down the hall to see if she heard any voices. She didn't. She tiptoed out, peeping Around every corner. No one is on site. She made it to the main suite and put her ear to the door for a listen. She heard the T.V. going but no voices. She slowly turned the doorknob to peek into the room. She looked over at the bed. No, Mike. She opened the door wider and saw his foot flopped over the chair.

Reign just shook her head at his life. Here, he was a ten-time champion of the world, and this is what he reduced his life to. Reign tipped into the room and stood over Mike. She knew he would feel her presence standing near if he was awake, like any other human. He didn't. He was out, and the loud snores confirmed that.

Reign strolled, surveying the room. Mike may have been on drugs, but she knew he wasn't broke. She knew he traveled with lots of cash and was determined to get some.

Her eyes jumped from one corner of the room to the other, and keeping a close eye on Mike at the same damn time. She had been around him enough to know he carried much cash in a black Louie V duffel bag. When her eyes weren't doing a good enough job, she began turning things over quietly, looking for that damn bag. She'd seen clothes, sneakers, shoes, and bingo in the bag. Reign was so excited that she ran toward the bag, no longer tiptoeing. She opened the bag and stared down at it. It was full of hundred dollar bills. There was no way he could know how much money was in this bag, she thought to herself.

She picked up a couple of stacks and returned them to the room with her. On her way out the door, Mike scared the shit out of her when he let out the loudest, stinkiest fart ever. She thought she was about to die. She held her breath and hurried out of the room before he woke. She returned to her room, dumped her bag on the bed, returned to the door to lock it, and put the chair up just in case. She took the money and started counting it. It was a lot. This was the most real bill she'd ever counted. It took her half the night to count.

She brought a bag of brand-new fruit of a loom crew socks and began neatly folding the money up in knots, rubber-banding it, and stuffing it in the socks. It was done so neatly that she didn't even understand how she made three hundred sixty thousand dollars look so neat. She sealed the bag back up and made it appear untouched.

She folded the outfits she had back up neatly in the bag, minus her underwear and pajamas, which she would need after a shower.

CHAPTER: 20

Token sat on her bunk, reminiscing about her future. She thought of everything she would do differently if God found it fit to free her. She wanted to change. She didn't want to leave there the way she went in, or even worse. She was thinking long and hard about what she was going to do. She knew it wouldn't be easy, especially after introducing this new lifestyle to her little sister. She thought of Reign constantly praying she didn't get caught.

She knew from experience that once you hit your first lick and get away with it, it would be hard to convince her that there was a better life than that. But the truth was, what was better than that? There wasn't a nine-to-five on this side of the earth that would pay them that money.

In Token's mind, it was worth it if you could make over one million dollars a year, and that's on a low scale for over five years or better, and you only get 3 to 5 years in the pin.

"INMATE DAVIS." Token jumped when she heard her name being called from the Bubble. She hurried off her bunk, slipped her state-issued crocks on, and made it to the C.O.'s station before the bitch grew impatient. "Yes, ma'am."

"Inmate, you must report to classification for a telephonic hearing." The token had no clue what the C.O. was talking about but hurried to classify if it was the news she'd been waiting for. Token got to Mrs. Adams's office and anxiously waited by her door for her to finish up a call. When done, she waved Token in and handed her the phone.

"Hello, yes. This is Token Davis."

Token's stomach did flip-flops at the sound of Ms. Blackman's voice. They weren't releasing her just yet. She just wanted to brief her on some things, but Token's hope grew with every word her lawyer said.

When the conversation was over, she handed Mrs. Adams the phone back and waited for her to be dismissed. Token damn near skipped back to her dorm. She was ready. Ready to hit the bricks. She was so close she could taste it.

"INMATE." She heard a familiar voice call out, and over two thousand inmates were on that compound. Token couldn't understand why the staff thought you'd know who they were talking to if they were all inmates. But for this voice, she knew she was the inmate he was referring to.

She turned around slowly and looked in Sarge's direction. He looked around in each direction before he flagged her over to him. She turned and walked in his direction.

This time, he didn't wait for her to get to him. He started walking toward a closed door. Token slowed her step as she watched him put his big key in the door and unlock it. He turned back around to make sure she was still with him. She was. When she got to the door, she realized she was in an old, dusty room that had not been utilized in what appeared to be months.

She was scared. The room was dark, and no one but the two of them were in it. "Sergeant, no disrespect intended, but it's recalled, and I don't want to get in trouble." Token's eyes met Sergeant's. "Now that is disrespect. How could you get in any trouble when you're with me." He leaned towards Token and kissed her on her lips. Token was shocked. She couldn't believe this man was putting the both of them in a situation that could get him fired and, even worse, get her sent to lock. Nevertheless, she went along with it. In her mind, it wasn't shit else to do.

Token almost forgot what it felt like to be kissed by a man—not just any man, but the sexiest one on the compound. His bowed legs made his uniform look even sexier than one could imagine. "Are you ready for me?" he whispered in her ear. "Because I'm ready for you," he continued.

"What if we get caught?" Token whispered as her pussy pulsated and wanted nothing but Sergeant to touch it. *Just feel it, she begged in her mind, for God's sake.* He has to have heard her because his hand made its way down to her pussy, sending her over the edge.

She was ready for whatever. She wasn't sure how much time they had, but she knew the count had just begun in that prison. There wasn't a C.O. on the site, so she knew they had at least thirty minutes or better. The kissing became more and more passionate. The two kissed like long-lost lovers.

"Are you ok?" Sergeant whispered in between kisses. While playing with Token's wet pussy.

"Fuck me, please," Token begged. The sergeant didn't hesitate. He whipped his dick out as if it was a direct order. He pulled Token's blues down to her knees and tilted her over; then, he stuck his dick in her. Her pussy was nice and tight, just as he had imagined.

Token's body was entirely of pleasure. It took her less than three minutes to cum. That shit was excellent to her. Once she came, Sergeant quickly followed. He pulled his dick out to nut on her ass cheeks.

He almost forgot to call in the one inmate that would screw up the count if she was not accounted for. Deeply winded and tired, he made that Call, hoping his voice didn't give them away. Count cleared. Token wiped her ass and headed back to her dorm with a double dose of happiness.

CHAPTER: 21

Chasity woke up the following day feeling overly exhausted. She didn't know why, but she didn't feel right. Something about her body felt different. She got up and pushed herself to get up and make things happen. She had to go to work whether she wanted to or not. She needed to be in the know.

Plus, she had yet to learn where Reign was and if she was in any trouble. It was time for her to start making more brilliant moves regarding her future. What if Token didn't come home? What if Reign got locked up, too? Where would that leave her? It was time she began to prepare for her future. She was getting all this money and had nothing to show for it? She paid Token's bills, her house, and a car note. Yes, she lived in the house and drove the car, but if they wanted to take it away, there would be nothing she could do about it, just like L.

She was not about to put herself in that same predicament that she just left.

The one thing she learned from Token and Reign is how to take care of yourself first. Chas finished getting dressed. She decided to put on something simple for the day. Her days of enticing Mr. Witterman were over. She wished his old ass crawled up under a rock and died. He was getting on her last fucking nerve trying to play her Daddy. When she would be in her office. He wouldn't hesitate just to come in and get his feelings on. It was welcomed at first, but once he promoted her and gave her a raise, there wasn't any more need for this activity.

He took her to a resort a couple of times, and although the place was beautiful and relaxing, having his old ass on top of her for hours trying to get it up was a headache. Chas finally arrived at her job. Everyone was huddled in the foyer with sad looks on their faces. She instantly knew something was wrong. She stopped to speak and find out what was going on. "If you haven't heard already, Chasity, we lost Mr. Witterman this morning."

Chasity took a deep breath. She tried to respond in a way that was expected. Everyone knew he favored her and expected her to be overwhelmed with sorrow. But the truth was she couldn't give a damn. She wanted him dead and out of her life. He was beginning to act as if he owned her, and that wasn't cool. Chas shed a fake tear and walked away with her face in her napkin.

This was wild. She just said how she wanted him dead, and poof, it happened. Now, she would be talking magic if she could make that money appear in her bank account and not get caught. Chas quietly took advantage of this time. Everyone was outside of her office crying and carrying on like the man was a saint. He was a scumbag, and they knew it.

Chas decided she was going get all she could before a new scumbag came in and made things a bit more difficult for her. She logged into the computer to open one of the accounts she created for wire transfers.

Once she noticed the coast was clear, she dropped one point two million dollars in the account. This type of activity wasn't an abnormal thing. Shareholders permanently moved their investments in lump sums. And since she was the only person doing some work, it was up to her to verify. Once the transfer was confirmed, she put on a show and acted like she couldn't handle being there anymore. The thought of Mr. Witterman's untimely death took a toll on her. She returned to where everyone congregated and gave everyone kisses and hugs goodbye.

They gathered around Her and told her to take as much time as needed. They would keep her abreast of the funeral arrangements. She wiped her eyes, said her goodbyes, and headed out the door. Unbeknownst to them, this was goodbye forever. Chas wasted no time getting her ass out of there.

She had plans, and this place was no longer in them. She pulled back up at the house and noticed no sign of Reign. She reached for her cell to try calling her again but decided against it. She figured wherever Reign was, she knew to call home. Reign knew Chas would be worried.

This was why she was sick and tired of giving her loyalty. She went to her room and packed a couple of things. Her nerves were wrong, and her stomach was doing flip-flops. This was the first time she had to make moves for herself in a long time. And she would take advantage of this opportunity. She grabbed her bag along with a picture of her, Token, and Reign sitting on her nearby nightstand. A tear ran down her face as she reminisced on this day at the prison. She took her bag and continued out the door, but only after dropping in an envelope with five certified checks totaling six hundred thousand dollars and a note. She didn't know how much money Reign owed on Token's defense, but she was pretty sure that would be enough and then some. Before exiting the home, she made one more stop.

The pups went wild when she kneeled to pet them. She loved her dogs but had to leave them behind. Where she was going, she needed to go alone. She cried some more. She cried to the cab that waited in front of the door.

When she got in, she asked the cab driver to drive slowly through the community, almost like she was in a funeral procession. In a sense, she was. The old her was dead and gone; she needed to find a new life. With all that money in her account, she knew it couldn't be that hard to make a new life for herself if ever she decided to go.

Reign had woken up to an empty hotel suite. The big fight was tomorrow, so she felt Mike was out training and hopefully getting groomed. She walked around the room and noticed it was still the same shit all over the place. She didn't want to have any parts of this foolishness. Reign called and tried to have her flight changed to an earlier flight but had no luck. The first plane that could switch wasn't until tomorrow, anyhow.

Since that plan failed, she got another room in a different hotel to stash her cash. The last thing she needed was Mike's people running through her things and finding the money she stole.

Once she put her things up at the Trump Taj Mahal, she returned to Ceaser's in no time, just like nothing ever happened. When she returned to the room, she opened Mike's door to see if the bag was still there. It wasn't. It was gone.

Mike took the bag with him, which was a plus for her. His team would never get to say she took his money while he was gone. Reign smiled to herself and went back into the guest suite, where she had spent last night, to order room service and a movie. When she picked up the phone, she could vaguely hear Mike coming in the door, laughing and talking to someone.

She turned the TV down and heard a woman's voice. Reign put the telephone back down and headed for the door. "Just where the hell do you think you're going?" Reign looked back at Mike as if he were the craziest person in the world.

"I'm leaving. You have company. Why in the world do you want me here?" The woman he was with looked confused. Reign didn't know who she was or why she was there, but she knew damn well the bitch wasn't a close relative.

Mike walked up to Reign and whispered in her ear. "Listen, little bitch I make shit happen for you and your sister. Now don't get all fancy and shit." He backed away, and then he came back in her face. "Don't bite off the hand that feeds you."

And he walked away, signaling his female counterpart to follow. She complied. Reign went back into the room to carry out her plan. She picked up the phone and dialed room service. With a craving for a sub of some sort, she ordered a hot pastrami and cheese with a Pepsi. The movie had been ordered and waiting for Reign to press play. She waited for her food. She heard a knock at the door; she hurried to answer it before Mike came out of the room. Judging from the sound, he was having too much fun in the other room to worry about her.

Reign got her tray and signed the receipt. She charged everything to the room and left a big enough tip for the room service woman to take off the next few days. She remembered an old saying that her Grandmother used to say. She would say the best way to hurt a man was to get him in his pockets. Reign was winning in that department. She had no worries.

She sat closed up in the room, watching *I Am Legend*. The noise from the other room grew louder and louder—the laughs, the moans, the talking—it was all sickening to her.

She still wondered why Mike would bring her here and did not want to be bothered. On the one hand, she wanted this question answered, but on the other, she didn't care. This was a grand opportunity for her. She could have all the cake and eat it too if she wanted to.

Suddenly, her stomach went roaring out of control. That had to be some lousy pastrami because she couldn't help herself. She dropped to her knees and began to crawl to the bathroom. She tried to call out Mike's name, but she knew he couldn't hear her.

She had turned up the TV so loud to drown out the sound of Bobby and Whitney in the other room that she drowned herself out, making it very difficult to hear. The pain grew more assertive. To Reign, it felt like someone was on the inside ripping out her uterus with their teeth. Reign couldn't take the pain. She made it to the toilet just in time.

She barfed up everything she had eaten today, yesterday, and probably the day before. She felt horrible. She had no clue as to what could have been wrong. She was hot and dizzy. This wasn't good.

All she needed was to be sick in Atlantic City with no one there to care for her. That would leave it up to Mike to care for her, and she didn't have that. Once she stood, she plugged the sink and ran cold water on it. She needed to shower but couldn't muster enough strength to get in, so putting her face in the water would suffice.

Reign couldn't figure out what was wrong with her life. Did Mike slip her something? All kinds of demented thoughts ran through her head. She reached over the toilet, pulled down one of the fluffiest bath towels she'd ever seen, and dried her face off.

After all, she was hungry again but too weak to eat. She lay down looking at the television screen but was more so looking past it, thinking about Token. Was this one of God's ways to get back at Reign for doing what she did to Token? She should not have been with him anyway. It wasn't planned. It just happened. When she first started going over to his house, it was innocent. There was no way in this world Reign plotted on Mike. He was more like a big brother to her. She confided in him. She knew he loved her sister, and that was all that mattered.

Everything was good until the day he asked her to take a swim with him. He started admiring her smile, beauty, body, everything, and Reign fell victim to it all. She knew she possessed all those qualities, but something about those words coming from him, a man, a famous boxer, made them feel more welcome. Not only that, Mike was there the night Reign was raped by members of his entourage and felt responsible. Plus, he didn't want any heat on his camp, so he slid Token as much money as necessary to make that issue disappear, and Token accepted.

When Mike told her that, she felt cheated; she had no idea what happened to her. She didn't know her sister had sold her off. Token had never given Reign any of the lavish gifts from Mike. She only gave her what she felt she should have and kept the rest for herself, leaving Reign curious to know what she could get. He promised to take care of her while Token was gone and protect her from the bad guys, but now Reign was confused about who the bad guys were.

CHAPTER: 22

The dorm was cold as fuck. Token walked in after count and headed straight for her bunk. Although it was live in there tonight, she wanted no parts. Movie night in B dorm was like chilling on the Ave. (so to speak). Everyone showered, fluffed their mats, and got comfy waiting for the main event. Not Token, she had other plans.

She first needed to put her rag on a showerhead to be in line for the next one. She needed to clean all that cum and shit out of her ass. She smelled like she'd been fucking. She only hoped that the nosy bitches that were in there didn't get a whiff.

Token was about to walk to the showers when she realized she had three envelopes on her bunk. She looked up at the big clock on the wall. She didn't know she'd missed a mail call. Receiving mail was like a main attraction. The dorm women would get very quiet when mail calls took place. If anyone spoke and caused someone to miss their name, they were liable to get their head knocked the fuck off. Token took a look at her mail. She just wanted to glance through it quickly, shower, chill out, and read it. But that was not happening. When she read the name on the envelope, she opened the letter and sat in her locker at the foot of her bunk.

"DAVIS!" Another inmate yelled, causing her to flinch. She looked toward the shower where the yelling was coming from. "YOU GOT NEXT," inmate Sanders wanted

to confirm. This shit was fundamental in the building. Every move was calculated. Every reservation needed to be kept. If you went out of turn, you were fucking up the line, and that was a no-no.

"NAWL, YOU CAN GO AHEAD." Token had just lost her spot, meaning she would have to return to the back of the line. She hated that because that's when the water was ice cold. Fortunately for Token, this was well worth it. She opened the letter and unfolded the page. What she read next was enough to melt her heart away.

My Dearest Token,

When this letter reaches you, I can only pray it finds you in the best health. I know you're surprised as hell to be hearing from me, of all people, but when I listened to what happened to you, it fucked me up for a minute. I was like, damn, how the hell did this happen. At first, I didn't believe it until my little sister sent me the article. Damn, Misses Money bags....You were doing it like that, shorty. (HAHAHA) Yeah, but no bullshitting. When I heard about the dude from Newark fucking you all over like that, I was feeling some way. I was ready to send that heat after him, so I'm glad he outed himself. I saved us a body.

Anyway, I'm not much of a writer. I just wanted to reach out to you and let you know that I thought about you a lot. I mean, even when I was on the block. It seemed like every time I wanted to push up, I couldn't. Something always stopped me. But let the truth be told, I was always digging you shorty. I always thought you were flying. A little intimidating but fly as fuck. I admired your hustle and always respected your gangster. I didn't know if you felt me like that, Dig. And if so, why did you never tell me? Of course, being in the belly of the beast, the walls talk, so you hear a lot.

I hope this note sheds light on things. I hope you understand where I'm coming from. I contacted Lil Sis to handle this; she put me on the game. Listen, kid, life is too short to be losing good friends. If I had a good friend, I probably wouldn't be in the shit right here (hahaha). Anyhow, I think you should reach out, and you all peace that shit up. She needs you shorty just like you need her. You are all bonded by some shit that's thicker than blood. You are all bonded by the streets. It's real out here. So when you get a minute, holla at cha boy. I might be here for a little minute, you heard. Stay cute, stay classy, and most of all, wait up.

Love your Boy

G-Money

When Token finished reading that letter, she was blown away, and so many years had passed. She couldn't believe it. It was G. The G. The love of her life, G. *"Omg"* was all she could think.

Although she was happy he contacted her, she was embarrassed at the same time. He wasn't supposed to know this part of her life. He was only supposed to see the good side. Now, all she thought of was how she would write back to him. She needed to find a clever way to do it like he found a way to write to her.

He had to want to talk to her. His letter had a forwarding address of her grandmother's house, which was pretty creative. She had to do the same thing and find a way to communicate with him. She wasn't as clever as he was. She didn't want to get caught. It was a rule in some jails. You could not receive mail inmate-to-inmate unless you were married, and if you got caught, you were going to the SHU.

"Davis, you're up!" the same inmate from earlier yelled. Everyone was showering and watching the movie, so Token had hot water.

Reign was in the guest suite fighting for her life. She didn't know when and how Mike got in, but he was in and blazing mad. She tried to make out what he was saying but couldn't. The blows to the side of her face made her hear. It was something about fools, money, and bitch. Those were the only words she could make out. Mike dragged her from one wall to the other, beating the shit out of her. His hands were like steel. It's a wonder that he didn't break her tiny neck.

She didn't beg or plead for him to stop. She just prayed quietly that God took her life. She didn't want to be hit anymore. However, there was no white towel to throw. It was over for her. Once the room turned black, she just knew her life had ended. Right there in Atlantic City, New Jersey, in the Caesar's Palace, where her name wasn't even the event's headliner.

ON ANOTHER NOTE

Her body was stricken with pain. Chasity landed in The British Islands. She needed to get away. She needed a fresh start. She chose this island because she knew she could transfer her money here, by a house with cash, and not be questioned about her former life. It was beautiful there. The Dutch were so caring and welcoming.

She figured she just wanted to live there for life. When she came out of the airport, the taxis waited. It wasn't like America, all rich and fancy, but it belonged to a proud cab owner who took pride in what he did. Unlike the states where you could tell if he made five dollars, he was proud of those five dollars and was happy to take them home to feed his family. That made Chas proud.

The first stop she made was at a bank. The greatest thing about this place is that they honor the American dollar, so she didn't have to go through the hassle of currency exchange. Even though euros and guilders are there, there's nothing like that good old Benjamin's.

She was already looking forward to this new living. The taxi driver pulled to a resort called Guana Island. That was where Chas would stay until she found permanent housing.

CHAPTER: 23

Reign woke up soaked in her urine. The sound of her cell phone woke her up, but she'd missed the call. "Jesus!" she yelled out. I should have never ordered that food.

First, it was the stomachache; then, it was the nightmares. Reign knew she needed to get out of that hotel room. She got up off the bed and grabbed her things to leave. This time there was no tiptoeing; she walked her ass out the door just as bold a lion. Mike had put no fear in her heart. Although the dream appeared accurate, he knew he'd better think twice before putting those hands on her.

While walking out of the door, she heard the party still happening in Mike's room. It looks as though more people have joined the free high program. This was the Pitts. The room looked like a crack house. No wonder he kept the do-not-disturb sign on the door. He knew they would have called 911 on him if he had gotten his room cleaned.

(Ding) A bell went off in Reign's head. As she made her way out, she pressed record on her cell phone, and you could hear Mike on his version of The GOP just having a ball. He wanted to play. Reign knew just what to do. She smiled as she walked by the living area, where empty crack vials with cocaine residue lay everywhere. She may have been young, but she wasn't a fool.

Reign closed the door before getting a clear view of the room number. Reign hustled to the Taj Mahal, where she'd booked her reservation and stashed her cash. She wasn't ready to leave A.C. just yet.

She walked down into the casino and watched people throw away cash. But not everyone. It was this young Italian guy who got her attention. He was cute, but that's not what intrigued her. What caught her eye was the amount of one-hundred-dollar chips in front of him. This shit was bananas to Reign.

The dude was placing thousand-dollar bets and winning. She was amused. She knew nothing of gambling, but from the way he made it seem, the shit couldn't be that hard. She stood close by ear, hustling to get at least the concept of it. She watched closely. She studied every move with her eyes. She figured she was a quick learner and had nothing to lose. When she thought she had enough knowledge, she went to her room to get cleaned up. She didn't want to come downstairs throwing money around, looking like an ordinary chick. She wanted to play and knew she would need to wear her big girl drawls and grow up quickly. This was the big league, and small people had no room.

Reign went upstairs and changed her clothes in two shakes. She returned to the stairs in due time and was ready to play. Because she'd thrown up all her food earlier, she felt a little light and thought it would be wise to grab a bite. She moved on over to the snack restaurant to grab her some wings. At the same time, she was keeping an eye on the young Italian guy who had now drawn a crowd over to his table. Reign stuffed herself as fast as she could to get to the table. She brought a wad of cash and was ready to turn it into a gold mine.

When she was done scarfing down the wings, she chased it with a Pepsi, giving herself much more energy. She stood to her feet and got a little dizzy. "What the fuck!" she did her best, coaching herself out of the spell. She waited for a minute before she took another step. A server came to her aid when she saw she was having difficulties. She went to get Reign a glass of water as she requested. Reign wasn't feeling well, but she leaned against the glass door, not taking her eyes off that table.

It wasn't like she wanted to rob him of anything. She just wanted to be a student. He moved with such poise while everyone around him was excited, overly excited about his winnings, while he remained calm. He was focused. Why, she didn't know. She thought the game was ten percent skill and ninety percent luck, so she didn't understand why he concentrated so hard. He had to have known something she didn't know, and she was determined to find out by any means necessary.

The woman had made it back just in time with the cold water. A white cloth accompanied her. Reign wasted no time dipping the fabric in her drink before putting it on her head.

She felt a sense of relief and shook it off by drinking the remainder of the water. Reign regained her composure, thanked the woman, and headed out the door.

She was back in business with an even better view. She sat two feet away from Mr. Lucky and ordered herself a drink. His luck was still rolling. She was surprised they didn't shut down the roulette table. She studied the guy, taking one mental note after the other. The one thing she noticed was the dealer spinning the wheel clockwise rather than counterclockwise. She didn't know much about the game but thought that was odd.

He hit again, and his fan base went wild. While he was cheering and had his hands in the air, he caught a glimpse of Reign—just as she had planned. She knew that if she sat in that seat, he would have a bird' s-eye view. He watched. She winked—not a desperate wink, but one that lets you know I see you.

There were more people gathered around. There was a head honcho that looked like an older version of the young Italian dude. He had to be his father. One could see the resemblance. He stood back watching, looking like a proud Papa. From the looks of things, this was a big-money family. Reign didn't know what they were into, but she knew she wanted in. She kindly tilted her head to eavesdrop on the older guy's conversation with a loan shark or bookie. She knew that because she heard them speak of a past bet.

She overheard the bookie-type guy boast about the elderly guy losing two million dollars because he bet against the Mexican. The Colombian would have beaten him, but he was disqualified for drug use. The conversations began to improve when they discussed tomorrow night's main event.

Reign damn near fell off the side of the chair, trying to hear this one. She listened to the older dude put his money on Tight Mike, and again, the Bookie-type dude clowned him. "Why do you always bet against the Mexican," she overheard him say. The two laughed and continued puffing on their cigars. At this point, Reign was no longer interested in the roulette game.

Unless it was Russian, and she got to pull the trigger while another mutherfucker held the gun to their damn head. Reign collected her thoughts as she hopped down from her chair, hurrying to return to her room. She stopped at the nearby table, where the men were standing, before trotting away arm and arm and picking up a card the older dude left underneath the ashtray. She didn't know whether it was faith or just plain luck, but whatever it was, she was more than ready to move forward with her plan.

Reign got back to her room and dialed the bookie dude's number. She was disappointed. It went straight to voicemail. She didn't want to appear desperate but needed to know the business. She kept her cell phone in her hand, dialing repeatedly, hoping she would get through before the night was out.

After trying for over one hour, Reign took her clothes off and got comfortable. She started feeling sick again and had a bad craving for oysters. She tried her hardest to ignore the craving by sucking her tongue. The taste didn't go away but kept her mind off of food and the matter at hand.

Reign picked her phone up and tried again. It rang. Now what. What would she say? How does she place a bet? Reign knew nothing about gambling but was ready to take her chances. The bookie picked up the phone and said everything Reign wanted to hear. You could tell this phone was used to place bets only. There was nothing formal about the phone call. He answered and asked if you had an account number already. If not, he gave you one. He let Reign know what the odds were and the minimal bet.

Reign played along like a pro. It almost felt like she'd done this before. She placed her bet and ended the phone call, only to add a new one. It was 7:30 AM the day of the main event. Reign had fallen asleep after being on the telephone half the night.

She was awakened by the television that sat nearby. This was the talk of all talks. Heavyweight champion Tight Mike Dickerson was caught in one of the most extensive drug raids in Atlantic City since the days of Midget Molley. It was significant, central, and cash in time. Because Mike violated the rules of the ABA, he was disqualified from the fight, arrested, and may endanger losing his already-earned titles.

This was a big payday for Reign. Her phone had several messages from the bookie, letting her know how to collect her dough.

She was excited but, at the same time, scared. No one on the outside knew she had called the police on Mike, but he sure as hell was going to see once they released those pictures that she sold to the tabloids. Reign's business was done in A.C. She had a plane to catch. She packed up her things and headed for the airport. If Token weren't ok by now, she damn sure would be soon.

CHAPTER: 24

Token's days were getting lighter and lighter. She pranced around doing the happy dance regularly, and days like this kept her hopeful. She had won her appeal and waited patiently for the judge to give her a bond hearing.

She hadn't heard from Reign, but Ms. Blackman assured her everything was fine. Reign had made every payment on time, and Token had owed her nothing. She began to like Ms. Blackman. Well, Mona was what she called her nowadays. From every phone call to every visit, it almost seemed they were family, not clients and council.

Mona had even worked out some favors for Token from the outside. They all waited patiently as God and Mona teamed up to work their magic. Token just waited patiently for the day to come.

Reign was so happy to be home. She pulled up her SUV to the driveway and got out. She looked around and frowned at the overgrown grass and the budding weeds. She knew she hadn't been home in a minute but damn. Chas could have called the lawn care people.

Reign walked in the door, and something was stinking as hell. It automatically caused her to take off running to a nearby bathroom to throw up whatever was in her stomach. The smell was beyond discussion. It smelled like death. When she came up for air, she put her face in the sink and ran it under cold water. This was becoming way too familiar for her. She found one of her t-shirts and wrapped it around her mouth as she walked through the house to see where the smell was coming from.

After two minutes of searching, the smell began to seep through her *nigga- rigged* mask. She made a beeline for the sink and pulled the door open, looking for anything to cover that smell. When all else fails, bleach will save the day. She pulled out the bottle and began pouring it everywhere. She poured it into a bowl, on the floor, and even on her hands so she could take a whiff now and again. She searched the house again, and bingo. It was the trash that was in Chas's room. "This nasty bitch. I'm in my good mind to call her ass right now and tell her off."

Where is she anyway? Reign searched the house but knew that was a waste of time. No way in hell could anyone have stayed in that house with that smell and lived to tell about it. On her way out the door, she noticed the letter Chas had left on the table for her. She was dying to open it and dying to get that trash out at the same time. With the letter in one hand and the garbage in the other, Reign walked outside and around the house to the trash bins. She started reading the letter. She knew something wasn't right when it sounded like a love letter.

This was too much for her. No Chas, no Token. Reign almost felt like she was brought there to suffer. She was returning to the house when a black van pulled up. It was late, so it caught her off guard. She tried to get closer to the door in case she had to run for it. That thought came and went too damn fast. Before she could move, a tall, oversized black man jumped out of the car and picked Reign off her feet. She was in a state of shock and could not scream. The man took her to the vehicle, where the driver was waiting viciously to pull off. The night was quiet. Reign had managed to kick off a shoe, leaving that as a clue as she was whisked away from there, never to be seen again.

I'M COMING HOME; I'M COMING HOME, TELL THE WORLD

"Token Davis, pack it up," the C.O. yelled from the bubble. This was the day Token would be Emergency Released from prison, but she wasn't entirely out of the woods just yet.

The judge had granted her release on bond to await trial for a second time. This was music to her ears. Mona had assured Token she'd never be back behind those walls again. At least, not in this case. Token walked around the dorm, giving away all her belongings she would never need again. She said her goodbyes and went to classification, where the clothes Mona had purchased were waiting for her to put on. She walked through the breezeway where she saw Sergeant.

You could tell he was happy to see her leave but hated to watch her go. Life was funny like that. She went into classification and got dressed. She hadn't worn real clothes in so long that she forgot what they felt like. She glanced in the mirror—*she had not seen one of those in a while*. She looked at the shape of her jeans in a *real* mirror.

Token brushed her hair back in a ponytail and was ready to take that walk. She could not wait to parade down the walkway where everyone could see her. The exit was located in the back of all the dorms. Everyone would get to see how fly she was in her street clothes.

Token paraded back through the compound for her final time. She walked by the Sargent one last time. He held his head down, not wanting to look, but when they made eye contact, he gave her the infamous head nod. Token made it outside the gates, where she could finally show real emotions.

Mona pulled her Beamer directly up the gate and jumped out to hug Token. The embrace was so natural. Tears streamed from Token's eyes, but it wasn't until she saw Mona's surprise that she would break down like a baby. Mona walked Token around the car and opened the left back door, and Cheeks sat there with the biggest smile ever. Mona didn't know how to keep that from Token but managed to. She felt that with all the bad news she had to give her in the past, with Chasity moving and Reign disappearing, she needed something to lift her spirits. Besides, they'd been back in touch for over a month. It was indeed time for Token's reign to be over and for her to turn over a new leaf............

ACKNOWLEDGMENTS

First, I have to give all the honor and all the glory to God, who makes it possible for me every day. To my die-hards….My boyz Carlton(CJ), Justin, and Elijah, you guys are my world. I have no clue what my life would have been like without you. To my husband, Jesse B. Kittles, I'm so glad God decided to bring us back together. You are my homie, my lover, and my friend. Although you get on my nerves sometimes, you only want me to succeed, so you push me the way you do. To my late great-grandfather Solomon Davenport, you have given so much of yourself to me. I will forever be grateful. RIP, and know I'm standing on God's promises. I love you to my grandmother Laura, my mother Denise, my father, the late Robert, my sisters and brothers: my family, The Davenports, Hawkins, Huntleys, and Simmons.

Since this book was written, God has blessed me with a beautiful Baby Girl, Jade Amor. Jade, you mean so much to me. This transition from a boy Mom has been easy because of your beauty. I love you.

If you are a part of a book club, please email me @Dimitakittles@gmail.com

Thank you all so much………. want to be a character in one of my books? Email me your thoughts on Token 1 and Token 2, and you'll be entered in a drawing…..

PLEASE SUBSCRIBE TO MY CHANNEL, DEFINITELY DIMITRA, where I discuss all of my books….